W9-APH-147

POODLE in the PANSIES

Ben M. Baglio

Illustrations by Ann Baum

Cover illustration by
Mary Ann Lasher

SCHOLASTIC INC.
New York Toronto London Auckland Sydney
Mexico City New Delhi Hong Kong Buenos Aires

ISBN-13: 978-0-439-02534-8
ISBN-10: 0-439-02534-6

12 11 10 9 8 7 6 5 4 3 2 1   8 9 10 11 12 13/0

Printed in the U.S.A.   40
First Scholastic printing, March 2008

Special thanks to Ingrid Maitland

One

"I *love* chocolate!" Mandy Hope declared to her friend James Hunter.

"Me, too," he answered, grinning. "Almost as much as I love school vacations!"

It was the start of spring break, and Mandy and James were walking home from the bus stop through the Yorkshire village of Welford. Mandy had just spotted a colorful Easter display in the window of the post office. Marshmallow chicks with licorice eyes peeked from a bed of green raffia grass; white and milk chocolate rabbits, temptingly creamy, dotted the scene. Planted on

1

sturdy chocolate feet, their long, smooth ears glistened in the soft spring sunshine.

"Yum," James said, hitching up his heavy backpack. "Days and days to do nothing but eat candy . . ."

Mandy laughed. "I hope the vacation will be more exciting than *that*! For a start, there's the village Easter egg hunt. Gran's organizing that, and I'm sure she'd appreciate some help."

"I don't mind helping. As long as I can sample the chocolate before we hide it!" James said.

Smiling, Mandy fell into step beside her friend. Spring was definitely in the air. A warm, fragrant breeze was blowing the last traces of winter away. New green leaves were everywhere; in the distance, on the rolling Yorkshire hills, she'd seen adorable woolly lambs dancing about on thin, wobbly legs. It was Mandy's favorite time of year.

Mandy's parents were both vets. They owned and ran the village veterinary clinic, Animal Ark. Mandy had grown up among animals of every shape, size, and species, and she loved them all. In her opinion, every creature who found its way to the clinic — from hamsters and parrots to owls and dogs — deserved the very best care she and her parents could give them.

As they reached the village green, Mandy noticed Ernie Bell, a retired carpenter, and his friend and neighbor, Walter Pickard, kneeling at the edge of a spectacular display of pansies. The circular bed was ablaze with purple, white, and lilac blooms.

"This one here," Ernie was saying as James and Mandy came up. "It's out of line, Walter. Do you see?"

"Hello," Mandy said, making Ernie jump.

"Hi there, Mandy," Walter Pickard said, looking up at her. "Could you and James take a few steps back and stand up on that bench, please? And tell me what you see?"

Mandy and James exchanged baffled frowns at the puzzling instructions. Then James dropped his backpack onto the grass and stepped onto the wooden bench. Mandy joined him. They peered down at the bed.

"It says, 'Welcome to Welford!'" Mandy cried. "Written in flowers!"

"It looks great," James agreed.

"You see?" Walter turned to Ernie and got creakily to his feet. "What did I tell you?"

"Are you sure?" Ernie called across the distance to where Mandy and James stood on the bench. "You don't think it doesn't look like *Welcome to Welfor*? Can you see the *D*? I don't think the flowers in that letter are doing their job."

"Yes," James called back. "I can read Welford."

Mandy jumped down. "It's fantastic," she said. She went over and put out a hand to help Ernie Bell to his feet. "It looks lovely."

"I'm glad you like it," he said, bending to brush the dirt off his knees. "A lot of work, but worth it. Walter and I have put a lot of effort into this."

"I'll have to keep Blackie away," James decided.

Mandy nodded. Unfortunately, it was too easy to imagine James's big, excitable Labrador trampling the delicate blooms.

"You'd better!" Walter pretended to grumble, wagging a finger at James. "Now, Ernie, if James and Mandy say they can see the *D* in Welford, then that's good enough for me. I think we've earned a cup of tea. Why don't you go on home and put the kettle on and I'll pop into the post office for some of Mrs. McFarlane's cherry jam. What do you say?"

"I say, OK!" Ernie answered. "Thanks for your help, you two. Bye!"

"Bye!" James and Mandy chorused. They heaved their backpacks onto their backs.

"I'd like a great big slice of white bread and cherry jam right now," James said.

Mandy didn't answer. Her attention had been taken by the sight of her father's Land Rover, slowing as he spotted her. He raised a hand.

"Hi, sweetheart!"

Mandy hurried over to the edge of the green. "Hi, Dad. Where are you off to?"

"Syke Farm," he answered. "There's a problem with one of the ewes. Do you want to come along? Hop in quickly if you do — I'm in a rush."

"Yes!" Mandy slung her backpack into the back of the car. James's landed on top of hers with a thud.

"Me, too," he said.

"Jump in, James," Dr. Adam urged.

Mandy and James scrambled into their seats and buckled their seat belts. Mandy felt a familiar rush of adrenaline. She loved going out on a call with her father or her mother, though she always hoped the problem they were attending wouldn't be a serious one. She and James knew the sheep at Syke Farm well; the farm was owned by Dora Janeki and her brother Ken Hudson, one of the shepherds in the Dales, and one whom the Hopes had often helped during lambing season.

"We've got a full appointment book back at the clinic, which is going to be tricky to juggle with all the spring lambs arriving. If only sheep were will-ing to have their babies all year-round!" Dr. Adam said, driving up the hill on the main road out of Welford.

"Spring break started today," Mandy reminded her father, "so we can help you as much as you want."

He glanced over his shoulder at her and grinned. "You can start right now! Check if my bag is fully stocked, will you, sweetie? I don't think I've used up anything I might need, but it's worth making sure."

Mandy tucked a loose strand of hair behind her ear and hauled her father's black bag into her lap. "OK, ready," she said.

"Iodine solution?" Dr. Adam asked, pulling up at a pair of bold iron gates.

"Got it," Mandy said as James got out of the car to open the gates.

"Syringe, antibiotics?" her father went on.

"Here," she said.

James shut the gates behind the Land Rover and climbed back in. They rumbled along a dirt road to the white-painted farmhouse up ahead.

Mandy went on investigating the contents of the bag. "And there's a roll of cotton cord and a lambing bottle. . . ."

"Scissors?" said Dr. Adam, easing the car to a stop.

"Yep," Mandy confirmed, brandishing them for him to see in the rearview mirror.

"Good, thanks," he replied. "All present and correct. Here we are." The Land Rover jolted to a stop on the paved yard behind the farmhouse.

The yard was streaked with mud from the recent rain, and loose pieces of straw were being whisked into the corners by the stiff breeze. On one side stood a row of box stalls, their top and bottom doors bolted shut. On the opposite side, there was a dilapidated open-sided garage in which a blue tractor was parked. The back door of the farmhouse opened and Ken Hudson, Dora Janeki's younger brother, came striding toward them, looking as though he was dressed for midwinter weather in a thick, hooded parka jacket. His

face was taut and pale, and his eyes looked very som-
ber. Tess, Ken's high-strung but loyal sheepdog, had
magically appeared to swirl around his feet. Her ears
were flat against her head, her tail down, as if she wasn't
sure about welcoming the visitors.

"Tess!" Mandy called, getting out of the car. She was
very fond of the beautiful black-and-white collie, having rescued her from a snowstorm one bitterly cold
Christmas. "Hi, Mr. Hudson," she added, looking up
from fussing over Tess. The dog pushed her sleek nose
into Mandy's palm and her feathery tail thumped on the
cobbles.

James gently smoothed her head. "Hi, Tess," he said.

"Thanks for coming out," Ken Hudson said, shaking
Dr. Adam's hand and leading him toward the field
beyond the yard. Mandy scurried to keep up and James
followed, with Tess trotting at their heels. Ken's big coat
billowed around him as he walked. In spite of the sun
shining out of a cloudless sky, the ends of a knitted,
fringed scarf trailed down his back.

"Why is Ken dressed for the Arctic?" James whispered, echoing her thoughts.

Mandy shrugged. Just then the farmer doubled over
in a fit of fierce coughing. "Oh, he sounds sick," she
whispered back. "Maybe he has the flu."

Ken Hudson led the way to the big barn. Inside, it was cold and dimly lit. Ken began to cough again.

"You don't sound well," Dr. Adam remarked.

"Just a pesky bug of some sort," he answered gruffly. "I can't take time off, not with Dora being away and the lambs being born."

"You're on your own on the farm?" Mandy's dad asked, sounding surprised.

"Just me," he confirmed. "Dora's gone to our cousin's golden anniversary celebration. The invitation just came at the wrong time!" He tried to smile, but Mandy could see the strain in his face. His eyes were red-rimmed and watery, as if being out in the cold wind had made them sore.

"Where's the problem ewe?" Dr. Adam asked, shifting his black bag to the other hand.

"It's Frida," Ken told him. "Over here. She's having trouble giving birth. There are two lambs to come, I figure."

The ewe lay on her side on a bed of clean yellow straw in one of the pens. Mandy had met Frida before and knew she could be a bossy, strong-willed sheep. But today she seemed a lot less confident. The sheep peered up mournfully at them with her slanted golden eyes. Because she had been sheared, Mandy could see her rib cage heave with each labored breath.

She kneeled beside the sheep in the straw while her father brought out his stethoscope. "Poor girl," Mandy soothed. "You're having a hard time, aren't you?" Frida glared at her and winced as Mandy laid a hand softly on her woolly head. Then she ducked out of the way to make room for her father.

"How long has she been in labor?" Dr. Adam asked Ken. He pressed the end of the stethoscope against Frida's ribs. The weary ewe made no attempt to get away from the cold metal disc.

"Several hours — over five, I'd say," he answered. "I haven't been keeping too close an eye on her because I've been busy with the other sheep. I'm afraid I'm not as prepared as I had hoped."

"Don't worry, Ken," Dr. Adam said calmly. But Mandy noticed her father's eyebrows crease up in a worried frown. She wasn't surprised he was anxious. Compared with other lambing ewes she'd seen, Frida didn't seem well! "It'll all be fine, I'm sure," Dr. Adam went on. "But it's cold in the barn — perhaps a little bit colder than what is good for newborns. Have you got a hair dryer we could use?"

Ken coughed again and fumbled for a handkerchief to put over his mouth. "I suppose Dora has one in her room. . . ." he mumbled. "Though I don't know why you'd need one. The roof isn't leaking; her fleece is dry. . . ."

"It's just a precaution, Ken," Dr. Adam said. "To warm her up a little while she's doing all the hard work. You've done a fine job so far," he added.

"I'll go!" Mandy said. She was eager to do something useful rather than stand around helplessly watching Frida suffer. She stepped away slowly from the stall, so as not to startle the ewe, then ran back toward the farmhouse. Tess was waiting at the door, lying on her stomach. The sheepdog twitched her tail in greeting, but there was no time to stop and pet her.

Mandy took the stairs two at a time. She had to open three doors along the landing before she found Dora's bedroom. She spotted the hair dryer at once, still plugged in and trailing its electrical cord across a wooden floor and up onto a glass-topped dressing table. She unplugged it and coiled up the cord so that she wouldn't trip during her sprint back to the barn. Tess sprang up when she burst out of the front door and shadowed Mandy across the yard.

She handed the hair dryer to Ken, who plugged it into an extension cord he was holding, then into a socket on a central wooden post.

"Where did Dad go?" Mandy panted, out of breath.

"Washing up," James told her. His chin rested on his forearms. He hung over the gate of the stall, frowning down at the exhausted ewe. "She looks really miserable," he murmured, and Mandy agreed.

Mandy's father reappeared. A strong scent of disinfectant hovered about him. "I'm going to have to help Frida along," he announced. "She's tired out. I doubt she'll have the strength to give birth on her own and you're right, Ken, there are two of them."

Mandy felt thrilled and fearful all at once. Twin lambs! Frida was struggling, and Mandy knew enough to feel alarmed; giving birth to one lamb was difficult, let alone two. Would Frida be able to cope with double the effort? The ewe's eyes rolled back in her head. She struggled to her feet, pawed at the floor, then lay down again, panting.

"Here we go," said James. Like Mandy, he'd watched lambs being born before and he knew the signs of imminent birth.

"OK, Frida," Mandy murmured. "Come on, girl, you can do it!"

Mandy watched a ripple of a contraction travel along Frida's lower belly. As much as she loved the sight of the sweet, scrunched-up, curly new lambs, she found the process of birth a little hard to watch.

Her father had pulled on a pair of long rubber gloves. He began to examine the ewe with one hand, pressing down on her spine with the other to keep her still. Bleating loudly, Frida tried to wriggle free and stand up.

Ken held on to her, his arms around her neck. But then a fit of coughing seized him and he stumbled. Mandy stepped quickly into the stall and took over. She kneeled behind Frida's head, wrapping her arms around the sheep's smooth neck. It took all of her strength to hold the ewe down and keep her still.

"Thanks, dear," Dr. Adam murmured, as Ken strode toward the door of the barn.

"I'll just get a drink," he gasped.

"He's *really* sick," James commented, watching him go.

Mandy's attention was on Frida. Straining and heaving, the ewe bellowed her discomfort.

"Don't worry," Mandy told her. "You're a smart, brave sheep. It'll be over soon."

Suddenly, a tiny lamb slid wetly into Dr. Adam's hands. As he laid it gently on the straw, Mandy let go of Frida's head to allow her to cuddle with her baby. The lamb was limp, gray-colored in the murky light of the old barn. Mandy's heart began to beat faster. Something was wrong! Frida turned her head away, rolling over onto her side and laying her cheek on the straw. She didn't seem at all interested in her lamb.

"Hair dryer!" Dr. Adam said urgently.

James handed it down. A noisy stream of warm air ruffled the tight curls on the lamb's small body. Dr. Adam cleaned its mouth and nose, then rubbed its ribs briskly with the flat of his hand.

"Here comes the second lamb," he said. "Mandy, can you help with this first baby while I see to his brother or sister?"

She switched places with her father and concentrated on stimulating the fragile little body, rubbing it, willing life into it, while holding the hair dryer at a safe distance. The lamb remained limp and still, its eyes closed. In her heart, Mandy knew it was no use. The tiny creature hadn't breathed at all. She felt tears well up and blinked them back.

Looking up, she watched her father deliver another stillborn lamb. The second limp body was even tinier than the first. Mandy saw the details of a sweet little face, its eyes tightly closed, and the beginnings of tiny curls along its small, woolly nose.

"Oh, no! Poor Frida," Mandy whispered.

The ewe's eyes were closed, her neck stretched out in the straw. She hadn't even bothered to investigate the latest arrival. She was suddenly free of the strain of her labor, and was resting, exhausted. Her breathing slowed.

"Sorry to have left you like that," croaked Ken, returning to the pen. "How's she doing?"

Dr. Adam looked up at him. Mandy had laid the lamb in the straw beside his sibling. The little creatures lay side by side, looking as though they were asleep.

"I'm sorry, Ken," said Dr. Adam.

Nobody said anything. Frida opened her eyes and lifted herself to nuzzle her twins, as if she thought that they might be alive after all. Mandy swallowed hard and got to her feet. James had walked away and was standing in the entrance to the barn, staring out at the sun-soaked field with its new shoots of bright, spring green.

"It's my fault," Ken said. "I should have known she was in trouble sooner than I did. I should have monitored her more closely. . . ." He trailed off, looking stricken — and Dr. Adam put a hand on his arm.

"Don't blame yourself! Sheep usually cope with twins perfectly well. There wasn't anything you could have done to save this little pair. You've got a lot to cope with here on your own."

Dr. Adam stood up and began gathering up his supplies. "Mandy, why don't you put the kettle on? We could all do with a cup of tea. James can help me bury the lambs."

Ken had another spasm of noisy coughing. "I'm not going to let this happen again," he rasped.

Mandy tucked her arm through Ken's. As much as she would have liked to help the dead lambs find their final resting place in the soft, dark earth, she could tell that Ken needed her support right now. "Come on," she said, "let's go and have some tea."

Glancing back, she saw Frida still pushing at the limp little bodies with her nose — and by the time Mandy was walking across the yard beside Ken, tears streamed freely down her cheeks.

Two

Waking the following morning, Mandy's eyes felt gritty from a bad night's sleep. Thoughts of Frida alone in her pen, while the other ewes gave birth around her, made her feel desperately sad. She pulled on her jeans and went down into the kitchen.

Dr. Emily looked up from the stove and smiled. "I was just going to call you. I made you an omelet," she said.

Mandy smiled her thanks and sat down. She poked the eggs around on her plate until the cheesy filling began to congeal.

"Not hungry?" her mother asked as she poured Mandy a glass of orange juice.

Mandy rubbed her eyes. She felt as if she had hardly slept at all. "Not really," she said. "I'm so sad for Frida and her lambs."

"It's very upsetting," Dr. Emily agreed. "Remember, though, that the lambs wouldn't have felt any pain. And sheep don't grieve in the same way that humans do. Frida will feel bewildered, but she'll soon recover."

"I hope Ken is going to be all right," Mandy added. "He's all alone on the farm, and more lambs will be arriving every day now."

"Most ewes handle things pretty well without any help at all," Dr. Emily reminded her. "It isn't often that things go wrong."

"But Ken is sick!" Mandy said. "He should be in bed."

"Dad and I will give him a hand." Dr. Emily came over to Mandy's side of the kitchen table and gave her a hug. "Don't worry too much," she said. "He's an experienced shepherd."

A sudden barking from outside the back door diverted Mandy's thoughts away from Frida. "Blackie," she said. "Walking James!"

Dr. Emily laughed and opened the back door. The Labrador bounded inside, his thick black coat shiny as glass. His tail waved in circles and, as Mandy bent to say hello, he licked her face with a warm, pink tongue.

"Or two, maybe?" James grinned. He snapped the leash onto Blackie's collar.

"No more bargaining. Off you go!" Dr. Emily ordered. "I'm going to help your father next door."

"Bye, Mom," Mandy said.

Her gran handed her a photocopied map of the village center. "Look for some really creative places, won't you?" she asked.

"We will," Mandy promised, and kissed her grandmother on the cheek before pulling the kitchen door closed.

Mandy had spent her whole life in Welford and she knew every nook and cranny of the village. "Pond Lane," she read, showing James a road at the edge of the map. "Let's start there."

"We need to hide the eggs in places where dogs and foxes can't sniff them out," James reminded her.

"Yes," Mandy agreed. "And not too high or children won't be able to reach them."

"Good thinking," said James.

Blackie was tugging him along, straining at his leash and making little coughing sounds. The village looked as if it just had woken up after a long sleep. Brilliant yellow daffodils nodded in the breeze; lacy pink blossoms drifted down like confetti from the trees. It all seemed brand-new, washed clean with color. Mandy felt her spirits begin to lift.

She waved to Walter Pickard as they passed the terraced cottages where he lived. He was sitting on a chair outside his front door, enjoying the sun. All three of his cats had joined him. Mandy could hear them purring as they got closer. Black-and-white Flicker was stretched out with her back feet on Mr. Pickard's waist and her two front paws over his shoulder while the other two cats each perched on a knee.

"Morning!" Mr. Pickard said cheerily. "I'm taking a well-earned break from gardening."

Mandy tickled Flicker under the chin, then stroked Missie and Scraps in turn. "We're on a mission for Gran," she explained, smoothing Flicker's head with her palm. Mandy was sure the cat remembered being rescued by her from the flooded river that had washed her in a barrel all the way to the doorstep of Animal Ark. The pretty cat always had a knowing and especially affectionate gleam in her eye when Mandy was around.

"We're finding places to hide the chocolate eggs for the treasure hunt," James added. Blackie had sat down. The Labrador was eyeing the cats through narrowed eyes, and James tightened his grip on the leash in case Blackie made a dash toward them.

"Nice day for it," Walter Pickard said. "Good luck. I promise not to watch you too closely."

"And no cheating!" Mandy said as Blackie jumped up, startling Missie, who hissed.

They walked on toward Pond Lane. Lots of people were out in the sunshine. Blackie's busy tail alerted them to Mrs. Ponsonby's approach. She was hurrying, out of breath, behind her two little dogs, Pandora and Toby. She seemed relieved when they stopped short to greet Blackie.

"I do *wish* they would slow down," she grumbled. "Mandy, dear, are you passing the mailbox? Would you take these Easter cards and drop them in for me? It's far too warm for Pandora to be out today. I don't want her to get overheated."

"OK." Mandy smiled. Honestly, Mandy thought, there was no pleasing Mrs. Ponsonby. It was either too cold or too hot for poor Pandora, who looked as if she were thoroughly enjoying the spring day.

"What are you doing out of school, anyway?" Mrs. Ponsonby queried, peering at Mandy and James from under her broad-brimmed floral hat. "Isn't it Friday?"

"It's spring break," Mandy explained.

"Oh, yes!" she said. "How nice for you. Well, I must get Pandora home for her rest. Thank you!"

Off she bustled, like a ship in full sail. James raised his eyebrows, and Mandy stifled a laugh.

James sighed. "We need to get to Pond Lane before there are any more delays."

"Right," Mandy said.

It wasn't far. At the end of the road was a small triangular-shaped patch of neatly mown grass, and Mandy spotted an ornate birdbath in a corner of it. James let Blackie off his leash and threw a stick for him to fetch.

"Here's a great place for an Easter egg," she called, pointing to a crevice in the base of the birdbath.

James came over. "Yeah, that's good. And I found a tree over there with a knothole in the trunk."

"That's two great places right here," Mandy said with satisfaction. She spread the map on the grass and marked it in the appropriate spots with two penciled X's. In tiny lettering, she wrote TREE and BIRDBATH.

"There's nowhere else to hide eggs along Pond Lane," James said. "It's all private property."

They walked on, looking out for other hiding places. Mandy suggested using the ledge of the top of a mile marker; James saw a spot in the wall of the church. They found a watering can, and Mandy thought the public telephone booth would be a great hiding place.

"Yes! We could slip the egg onto the shelf where the phone book is," James said. It would be easy to spot but not everyone would be good at looking for the eggs. It would be great to give even the youngest competitors a chance of finding one.

"We've found tons of places," Mandy said, looking at the map, which was now covered with small sketches and penciled notes.

"It's time we claimed our reward," decided James, patting his stomach.

They had walked in a circle and were back near the village green. Blackie had found a bowl of water outside the door of the post office and was lapping thirstily. While she and James waited for him to finish, Mandy heard the clip-clop of hooves. She turned to see Tania Benster walking Gabriel, her miniature pony. The adorable pony was too small to be ridden by anyone bigger than a very young child but he loved going for walks on a lead rein, just like a dog.

"Hello," Mandy called. She ran over to pet the pony. His mane was looking thicker and tuftier than ever and his coat gleamed. Tania must have given him a special grooming for his outing today.

Tania tugged on Gabriel's rein to halt him and he snorted. "Hi, Mandy." She waved to James, still waiting for Blackie outside the post office.

Mandy patted Gabriel and moved his forelock out of his eyes. It was black and very long, like his tail, which almost touched the ground. "Hi, sweetie pie," she said.

"He's grumpy," Tania said. "He's on a diet because the spring grass is too rich for him and he misses his treats."

"Oh, poor Gabriel!" Mandy laughed. "If horses could eat chocolate I'd save you an Easter egg! My gran has bags and bags of them. She's organizing an Easter egg hunt for next Sunday, and James and I have been looking for secret places in the village to hide them," Mandy explained.

"That sounds like fun! Gabriel would be happy to dress up and give rides to little kids on the day, if you like," Tania offered. "He loves that kind of thing!" She rubbed the pony's forehead and he whickered softly.

"In return for a treat? I'll find something healthy, like carrots!" Mandy smiled. "What a good idea."

"OK, it's a deal. I'll get my mom to call your gran about when we should be there," said Tania. "I'll go and start planning our outfits right now!"

"Thanks, Tania!"

James was coming over with Blackie, whose whiskery muzzle was dripping wet. Suddenly, there was a shout from behind them. Mandy spun around, gazing toward the green.

"Look at *this*!" Ernie Bell bellowed, waving his arms. He was very red in the face and his cap had fallen onto the grass beside him.

Mandy hurried toward him with James and Blackie close on her heels. "What happened?" she asked.

Ernie pointed to the bed of pansies he and Walter Pickard had worked so hard on. "Ruined!" he announced dramatically.

The flowers that had so magnificently spelled out WELCOME TO WELFORD had been trampled to a soggy purple-and-white carpet. A hole had been dug in the middle of the bed of blooms, revealing pale pansy roots and a few worms wriggling frantically to get underground once more. The whole bed was a mess of loamy earth and torn petals.

"Oh, no!" Mandy gasped.

Ernie Bell looked suspiciously at Blackie, who looked up at him and wagged his tail. "Was it you?" he demanded. Blackie's tail stopped wagging.

"No!" James protested. "It couldn't have been Blackie. He's been with me the whole time."

"Could it have been Gabriel?" Mandy wondered.

"Gabriel who?" Ernie prompted. "Where does he live? I'll go and have a word. . . ."

"No, no, I was just wondering about Tania Benster's pony. He's on a diet and I guess he might have been hungry enough to eat the flowers. . . ." Mandy stammered to a stop, wishing she hadn't mentioned poor Gabriel. After all, she knew Tania never let him off the lead rein when they were walking around the village. Ponies weren't like dogs, and didn't always come back when they were called.

Just then, a fast-moving blur of pale, curly fur shot across the green and dived into the remaining pansies. It rolled around luxuriously on its back, kicking up determined little legs and grunting with pleasure.

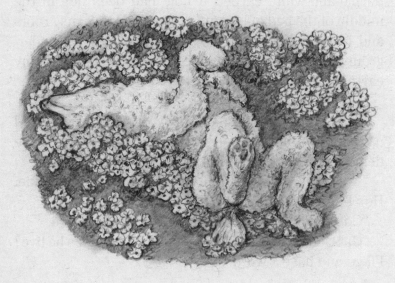

"There's the culprit!" James cried triumphantly.

"Shoo!" shouted Ernie, flapping his arms.

Mandy tried hard not to laugh. Ernie Bell was clearly upset about his ruined display and she did feel awful for him. But the cute little dog was having a wonderful game in the pansies — and it was the prettiest apricot-colored poodle Mandy had ever seen!

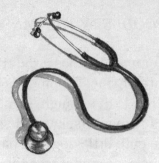

Three

"Here, girl!" Mandy called. "Come! Come!" She clapped her hands to attract the dog's attention.

Blackie was straining at his leash, eager to jump into the pansies and meet the poodle.

"No, Blackie!" James begged, trying to hold him back.

The little dog stood up and looked at Mandy with her head on one side, pricking her tiny, triangular ears. She wagged her short, fluffy tail, then bounded over to say hello.

"You're so *cute*!" Mandy whispered, not wanting to upset Ernie Bell by praising the adorable vandal. The dog was a medium-sized female, with a curly, pale, peach-colored coat. Two intelligent brown eyes searched Mandy's face, then she stood on her hind legs and licked Mandy's hands with great affection. Mandy scooped her up in her arms. The dog was a miniature poodle, about the size of a spaniel, so she was a little awkward and heavy to lift off the ground, but she seemed very happy to be hugged.

"Where's your owner?" Mandy wondered out loud, looking around. The poodle was investigating her ear, snuffling sweetly. She was clean and well fed; Mandy could just feel her ribs through her soft fur and her coat smelled faintly of dog shampoo. The little creature had such an adorable personality that it wasn't surprising she was obviously someone's much-loved pet. Mandy held the dog closer and kissed one fluffy ear.

"Yes, where's its owner?" Ernie Bell demanded, still sounding miffed. "I'd like to have a word with him about controlling his dog!"

"I don't know," Mandy admitted. "I've never seen this dog before, Ernie."

James had come over. "Maybe she's lost?"

"Well, she doesn't look like a stray, so there must be someone close by looking for her," Mandy told him. "Isn't she the cutest thing you've ever seen?"

Ernie Bell began to calm down. "She is a pretty little dog," he agreed. He put out a hand to the poodle, who wagged her tail, content in Mandy's arms. It was such a relief to come across a stray dog that was in a healthy condition. Mandy had rescued dogs before — like the beautiful Dalmatian Dapple, who had been in a terrible state of neglect when she was abandoned.

She smiled at Ernie. "James and I will help you and Walter to fix the flower bed, I promise. Just give me time to find the dog's owner, OK?"

Ernie gave a big sigh. "No, don't worry. It's not your fault. Walter and I can do it. I suppose it won't take too much to get it back the way it was," he said, shaking his head and surveying the flower bed. "I'll get Walter and we'll get to work. But it *is* a nuisance."

"It is," James agreed, nodding. "I'm sorry, Ernie."

"James, will you come with me to see if we can find out where she came from?" Mandy asked. "We haven't much to go on. She's not wearing a collar."

She put the poodle down, and Blackie towered over her, his tail wagging madly. The dog sniffed Blackie all over, looking friendly and confident. She was clearly used to being with other dogs. Mandy took off her soft cotton belt and tied it loosely around the poodle's neck as a makeshift leash.

"Come," she said, pulling her gently along.

They walked around the green and set off along the main road through the village. The poodle was content to trot beside Mandy, walking obediently to heel, her tail high. At the post office, James called through the open door to Mrs. McFarlane.

"Yes, James?" she said, taking off her glasses and leaning forward on the counter. "Oh! Mandy, what have you got there?"

"She's a miniature poodle," Mandy explained. "And she seems to be lost. Has anybody asked about her?"

Mrs. McFarlane shook her head. "Not a soul," she said. "And I've never seen her before — I'd definitely remember such an unusual color. What a cutie!"

"She is," Mandy said, bending to pat the poodle's head. "Oh, well . . . will you let us know if anybody asks about a lost dog?"

"Right away. Good luck," she replied.

"It's a mystery," James said as they headed back toward Animal Ark. "I mean, she's a great-looking little dog. And she's in good shape."

"She hasn't been mistreated," Mandy agreed. "There must be someone who's trying to find her."

"Well, then," reasoned James, "Animal Ark is probably the best place for her to be. If I'd lost a dog around here, I'd go to the veterinary clinic, wouldn't you?"

"Yes, I would," Mandy said, adding, "but we'll make some flyers and put them up around the village just in case."

"We're going to need a photograph of her, then," James said. "I'll go home and get my camera. I'll come over after lunch, OK?"

"OK," Mandy agreed.

When she reached Animal Ark, she was happy to see that there was only one car in the parking lot with their Land Rover. That meant her parents wouldn't be too busy, and one of them would be able to examine the poodle to make sure she was in good health.

"I think we'll call you Sunshine," she told the poodle, ushering her through the door into the clinic. "Your coat is the exact color of a sunrise!"

As Mandy shut the door behind them, Sunshine stopped short, sniffed the air, and began to quiver. Simon Weston, Animal Ark's nurse, was chatting with the receptionist, Jean Knox, at the front desk. They both looked up. Jean frowned and pushed her glasses up onto her forehead.

"Oh, Mandy," she said, peering at the floor over the desk, "what have you got there?"

"Hello!" Mandy greeted them. "This is Sunshine. I found her on the green. I think she's lost. No collar, and nobody we've asked so far seems to know her."

Simon came over. "Hi there," he said, bending down. "You're a pretty girl."

Sunshine looked at him. Her tail was down and her ears trembled. Simon stroked her. "Hey, it's OK. We're not going to hurt you."

"Oh, poor Sunshine," Mandy said. "She's really nervous."

"I bet her owners will turn up," said Jean. "Your dad's finishing up in room three, so you can go straight through to see him. Your mom's in the kitchen. She just came in from checking on a sick lamb."

"She looks like a great little dog." Simon smiled. "I'm sure you'll soon find out where she came from, Mandy. Good luck!"

"Thanks, Simon." Mandy lifted Sunshine into her arms. The poodle snuggled up tight against Mandy's chest, pressing her little woolly head under her hair, hiding her face.

"Dad!" Mandy said, pushing open the door to the treatment room with her foot.

Dr. Adam was wiping down the examining table. "Yes?" he said. "Oh, who's this?"

"She's lost, I think. She dug up Walter and Ernie's pansy bed on the green. James and I went around asking, but nobody knows her." Mandy lowered Sunshine onto the table. Her nose twitched and she trembled even more, until the little tuft of peachy hair at the tip

of her tail quivered. Mandy steadied the poodle with a firm, soothing hand, but Sunshine's feet scrabbled madly on the shiny metal surface.

"At first glance, she seems OK," said Dr. Adam. "Let's get a good look at you, OK, pooch?"

Sunshine dropped down into a crouch. She peeked up at Dr. Adam through a fringe of cream-and-pale-orange fur. She was tense. Mandy knew that many dogs felt nervous in vet clinics — not because they were afraid of being hurt but because they didn't like the smell of disinfectant. Very gently, Dr. Adam lifted Sunshine's face and looked at her gums, which were a healthy pink.

"She looks like a purebred apricot miniature poodle," he announced. He looked at her teeth. "About a year and a half old, I'd say."

"She's gorgeous," Mandy said, running her hand down Sunshine's spine. "Somebody must love her."

"Yes, she's healthy," her father agreed. "I can't find a single minor wound. No scratch or scrape of any kind." He felt Sunshine's tummy. "No abdominal problems. She's not thin, either." Mandy watched and waited. "Her ears are clean — not a mite in sight. Her coat is in great condition, too."

"Well, that's good news." Mandy smiled. "I'll put up some posters, in case her owners don't realize they can come to the clinic to look for her. James will help me.

But, Dad, can I take her to the house? I don't want to leave her in the residential unit. She doesn't seem to like being in here one bit!"

Sunshine chose that moment to stand up on her hind legs and lick Mandy's face as if to say, "Yes, please!"

Mandy's father laughed. "How can I say no?"

"Good! Thanks, Dad," Mandy said, adding, "I'm going to call her Sunshine, just until we find her owners."

"OK. You start making some flyers," he said. "I'll make some phone calls to colleagues, too. Let me just run a scanner over her in case she has a microchip."

Sunshine sniffed curiously at the small machine as Dr. Adam passed it over her. The scanner hummed lightly around her head, and Dr. Adam concentrated on Sunshine's ears, but there was no identifying chip to be found.

"Nothing," he concluded. "Well, give her something to eat and drink —"

Jean Knox put her head around the door. "Dr. Adam?" she said. "Ken Hudson is on the phone. Can you take the call?"

"Yes, thanks, Jean, put him through," he answered.

Mandy lifted Sunshine into her arms. She felt strongly that all pet animals should be microchipped for identification purposes. However, she couldn't help feeling a tiny bit relieved that Sunshine *didn't* have a microchip because it meant Mandy would be able to spend some more time with her. She didn't want to have to say good-bye to the pretty poodle just yet!

She turned to leave as her father picked up the receiver. She heard him tell Ken not to apologize. "It's really no trouble at all, Ken. No, we're not too busy, and we've got some milk supplement."

Mandy hovered in the doorway, patting the poodle in her arms. She listened nervously, thinking about Frida and hoping it wasn't more bad news from Ken.

"I'll bring it up to you right away," her father was saying. "Don't worry, really."

"What is it?" Mandy asked, frowning, as he put down the phone. "Is everything OK?"

"It's fine. Ken needs some milk supplement. He wants to be fully prepared in case any new lambs need bottle-feeding," Dr. Adam explained. "He's been too busy to get to the store, and lambs are coming thick and fast. I'm going up there now."

Mandy felt torn. She wanted to go to Syke Farm with her father and see Frida and the newborn lambs, but that would mean leaving Sunshine.

"Coming?" Dr. Adam asked. He smiled. "Simon will watch the poodle for a while, I'm sure. We're not busy."

Mandy looked down at Sunshine. Her eyes were closed, her cheek resting on Mandy's forearm. "She's tired," she realized. "I'll take her to Simon, and when we get back, I'll take her into the cottage and make her a cozy bed to sleep in. Give me two minutes."

Ken Hudson waved from the door of the big barn when the Land Rover drove up, then vanished back inside. Tess, lying down at the entrance, got up and wagged a shy tail in greeting. Mandy admired the dog's patient obedience; she knew she wasn't allowed in.

Inside, the barn was warmer than it had been the day before. Small, determined bleats rose up from the pens on either side of the walkway.

"Shut the door, will you?" Ken called hoarsely. "I've got a couple of electric heaters on in here."

"How's it going, Ken?" Mandy's dad asked. She followed him down the central aisle, her head turning left and right as she peered into the pens, hoping to catch a glimpse of some new lambs.

"Pretty well," Ken said, his voice muffled by a thick woolen scarf. He was laying out fresh straw, shredding it from a bale around a heavily pregnant ewe. Ken was flushed and feverish; Mandy could see two round spots of high color on his cheeks. A thin film of sweat glistened on his brow. He looked even more sick than he had the day before.

"Can I do anything to help, Mr. Hudson?" she asked.

"Milk supplements?" Ken seemed to gasp the question.

Mandy's father quickly reassured him. "They're in here," he said, and tapped the box under his arm.

"Thank you," Ken said. "That's very good of you. I'll just finish here." He went back to his work, and Mandy took the chance to slip away. She found Frida in the same pen as before, pressed up against the gate. Mandy thought she looked about as miserable as a sheep could. The big ewe was staring across the walkway to a pen where a new lamb was being cleaned by its proud mother. Mandy put a hand out to her but Frida grunted and moved away. She sniffed the floor of the stall where her twin lambs had been born, then walked around, nosing the straw, as if she was searching for her babies. Mandy's heart ached for her. There was nothing she could do to help Frida.

She would offer to make Ken a cup of tea, she decided. At least she could be useful that way.

"I'll go and make up the formula for you, Ken," she heard her father telling him. "I'll put it in the fridge in your kitchen, OK?" Mandy heard him chatting to Tess as he crossed the yard to the Land Rover. "Yes, you're a good girl!"

"Your dad's a great help," Ken said, pouring fresh water into the trough from a bucket.

"Would you like some tea?" Mandy asked.

Ken stood up and pressed his hands into the small of his back. *He is very pale*, Mandy thought.

"Well, yes, I would. Thank you, Mandy," he said. Suddenly, she saw his face tighten into a grimace. He staggered and fell back onto the ewe, who bolted, bleating in alarm. Ken collapsed into the straw he had carefully laid for the lamb's arrival. He lay on his side, unmoving.

"Oh! Mr. Hudson!" Mandy cried. "Dad? *Dad!*"

She jumped into the pen and kneeled down in the straw. She lifted the farmer's head, propping it up on one of her knees. "Dad!" she yelled, hoping she wasn't frightening the sheep. Her heart was pounding with fear. Had Ken Hudson died? Should she leave him lying on the floor and go for her father?

"I'm here," said Dr. Adam, and Mandy looked up and felt relief flood through her. She stood up shakily. Her dad climbed into the pen and calmly took over. He knew exactly what to do, so Mandy stepped back and watched gratefully. Dr. Adam rolled Ken onto his back. Ken gave a low moan when his shirt was unbuttoned and the cold, steel disc of Dr. Adam's clean stethoscope made contact with his chest.

"His heart is strong," Dr. Adam told Mandy. "I think he has pneumonia. He needs to see a doctor."

Ken blinked slowly. His white lips moved, and then he gave a puzzled frown. "What happened?" he asked, looking up at Dr. Adam.

"You're very sick, Ken," Dr. Adam explained. "I'm going to drive you to your doctor."

Ken sat up and shook his head. "No," he said. "That's kind of you, but I can't leave the farm. The sheep . . . There's no one else."

Dr. Adam helped Ken to his feet and hung on to his arm. Dr. Adam obviously wasn't going to let the farmer argue. Mandy took his other arm. They left the flustered ewe, still bleating, and led Ken out to the Land Rover. As they crossed the yard, Tess ran in low circles around her owner, looking up adoringly at him. Mandy wished she could pause and offer the sheepdog a little affection, but she didn't dare let go of Ken Hudson's arm.

Her father urged Ken onto the front seat of the car. There was a blanket in the trunk that Mandy got and she laid over his knees. He was shivering.

"Are you comfortable?" she asked.

"I'm fine," he said gruffly, fumbling with the blanket. "Stop fussing, now! You're kind, but, really, I can't go right now. I'll make an appointment to see the doctor next week, when Dora gets back."

"No," Dr. Adam said, "I'm taking you now, Ken. I'll call Jack Spiller at Fordbeck Farm and ask him to keep an eye on the sheep. He and his wife, Maggie, have a veterinary student cousin staying with them who can take care of their flock. Either Jack will help you out, or the student will. Or I will! Somebody will help, I promise. Now, let's get you to that doctor, OK?"

Mandy got into the back of the car. Ken sighed and let his head fall back against the seat. "I am very tired," he admitted.

Dr. Adam started the Land Rover and turned it in a wide circle on the gravel drive. Mandy saw Tess's ears prick up. She trotted after the car for a while, then, as the vehicle picked up speed, she began to race full tilt after them. The dog kept pace alongside the rear wheels until Dr. Adam reached the gate to the main road, where Tess stopped. She sat down, panting, and gazed forlornly after the car until Mandy could no longer see her.

Poor Tess! she thought. *Poor, sweet Tess!* She knew that her father would make sure that someone stepped in to help Ken out, but meanwhile lambs were still being born, and there would be no one at the farm for at least an hour. Oh, what a time for Ken to get sick!

Four

By the time they reached Dr. Mason's office, Ken Hudson had fallen asleep. His head lolled, and even the lurching of the car didn't seem to disturb him.

"I'm so glad you heard me yell," Mandy told her dad quietly, leaning forward and putting a hand on his shoulder. "I didn't know what to do."

"You did exactly the right thing," her dad told her. "You stayed with Ken and shouted for me. He's going to be fine once he gets medical treatment."

There were several people in the waiting room but Ken was rushed in to see the doctor right away. Dr. Adam went back out to the parking lot to make a call to

Jack Spiller. Mandy leafed through a magazine. It had an interesting article on traditional blacksmith techniques, but she was too worried about Ken and the sheep to concentrate.

At last, Ken shuffled out into the reception room, looking very troubled and pale. Dr. Mason followed him.

"Dr. Hope?" The doctor scanned the faces of the waiting crowd, just as Mandy's father stepped back inside.

"Yes?" he said. "Hello, Dr. Mason."

"Hello! I'm so glad you were at Syke Farm this morning! I'd like Mr. Hudson to go into the hospital for a few days. He has pneumonia and needs complete rest. Could you take him over to Walton Hospital right away?"

"Of course," said Dr. Adam.

"Look, I keep telling you," Ken said, turning to the doctor, "it's impossible for me to leave the farm right now."

Dr. Adam held up a hand. "It's all taken care of, Ken," he told him. "Jack Spiller is on his way over to the farm right now, and he'll stay until you're well again. The sheep will be in excellent hands."

Ken looked suspicious. "But what about my Tess?" he growled. "She doesn't take to strangers."

"I know that," Mandy's dad answered. "But your health is more important than anything else. You'll be no good to Tess or the sheep if you get any sicker. And Jack will make sure she's safe and fed."

"I guess you're right." Ken gave in and gave Dr. Adam a crooked smile. "Thanks," he said. "Thank Jack Spiller for me, too."

Relieved that it had been settled, Mandy linked her arm through Ken's and walked slowly with him back to the car. She put the blanket over his knees again and on the way to the hospital, she told him all about Sunshine. Ken stayed awake, but he didn't say much in return.

The head nurse, Marion Timpson, who was a friend of Mandy's grandmother and knew Ken, took charge of him as soon as they arrived at Walton Hospital.

"Hello, Dr. Adam. Hello, Mandy!" she chirped. "What have you done to Ken, poor man? He looks pretty bad!"

"I had to leave Syke Farm, Marion," Ken told her. "Right at the start of spring! What a time to be sick!"

"Now, don't you worry about those sheep of yours," she replied. "Sheep know what they're doing — they've been doing it for years, and they'll go on doing it with or without you."

She ushered Ken into a comfortable room that overlooked a small courtyard garden. Mandy thought it looked like a nice place to have a rest. Marion shooed Mandy and her father away with a flap of her hands. "Rest is what he needs," she said. "Both of you go away now and let the man sleep."

"Wait!" Ken called as Mandy turned to go. "Tess's food — she likes her dog food dry, remember. It's in the garage, in a metal can."

"Don't worry," Mandy said. "I'll tell Jack Spiller. You just get well. We'll take care of everything for you." Then she had a sudden thought. "I can bring Tess in for a visit!"

"No dogs in my hospital!" Marion frowned, but Mandy grinned.

"Twinkle came, remember? The little Jack Russell terrier who made the patients laugh at Christmastime?"

"Well . . ." Marion said, "he was an exceptional dog, Mandy. Very well behaved!"

"Tess is a great dog, too," Dr. Adam put in impishly.

"Maybe I could bring Tess into that little garden?" Mandy persisted, pointing out of the window.

Marion smiled and wagged a stern finger at Mandy and her dad. "We'll see," she said. "Now, off you go, both of you!"

Mandy waved at Ken. "Bye," she said. "Don't worry about a thing. Just rest and get better."

Dr. Adam put a hand on Ken's shoulder. "I'll bring you some things from Syke Farm. Maggie Spiller will help me find them. Pajamas, toothbrush, a book to read, that kind of thing . . . OK?"

Ken nodded without looking around. He was sitting on the narrow hospital bed, staring out at the flowers in the garden. Mandy felt very sad for him. He had always been a small man, but on the farm he seemed strong and wiry as he heaved sheep around and repaired walls. Now he looked frail and defeated, as if he would have to struggle to lift the tiniest lamb. Mandy wished she knew him well enough to go over and hug him, but she knew that would startle him. Instead, she waved to him once more, then she and her dad left him to Marion's efficient care.

Pulling into the parking lot of Animal Ark, Mandy saw James's bike propped up against a wall. Her father let her out, then left again immediately to drive up to Syke Farm to meet Jack Spiller and get a bag of things for Ken. Mandy hurried into the clinic. She was eager to see Sunshine and hoped James hadn't been hanging around waiting for her for too long.

The poodle was just inside the door, her tail wagging. She stood up on her hind legs and licked Mandy's hands as she bent down to pet her.

"Sunshine!" she said, delighted. "Have you missed me?"

"She has!" Simon laughed. "I think she recognized the sound of your dad's Land Rover. She rushed from the back of the clinic to the front and tried to look out of the window, but she's too small to see over the sill."

Mandy sat down on the floor and allowed Sunshine to get into her lap. "You're a smart girl," she told her. She stroked the poodle, who snuggled up close to Mandy's chest, then lay down with a contented sigh. "Hey, don't get too comfortable!" Mandy warned. "I need to find James."

"James is next door with your mom," Simon said. "He arrived with his camera a while ago."

"We're going to take a picture of Sunshine for the flyers," Mandy explained. She lifted Sunshine off her lap and stood up. "Maybe we'll photograph her outside. Thanks for watching her, Simon."

"No trouble," he said. "She's a great little character."

Mandy let her trot along through to the cottage's kitchen. Her mother was buttering a scone for James.

"Strawberry or apricot?" Dr. Emily was saying. "Oh, hello, honey!"

"Apricot," James said. He looked over as the door to the clinic closed. "Mandy, where have you been? Hello, Sunshine . . . speaking of *apricot*!" He leaned down and ruffled her fluffy coat.

"Sorry, James. It was an emergency. Dad and I had to take Ken to the hospital. He's got pneumonia," Mandy reported.

"Pneumonia!" James echoed, raising his eyebrows.

"Dad called me from the car a minute ago," Dr. Emily said. "I'm so sorry for Ken. I expect he's been working far too hard since Dora left."

"Poor Mr. Hudson," James agreed. "I'm worried about the sheep, too."

"Adam arranged for Jack Spiller to help out while Ken's in the hospital," Dr. Emily said, standing over James with a teaspoon and a jar of jam.

James held out his scone. "Thank you," he said. "How long will he be in the hospital?"

"About a week," Mandy said. "He doesn't like the thought of abandoning the sheep — or Tess."

She looked down at Sunshine, who looked back at her with a bright, steady gaze. The curls on the top of her head were gorgeous, Mandy thought. They were a soft, creamy color that contrasted beautifully with the pale orange of her cheeks and chest. She hadn't been clipped in the classic poodle cut, which left a dog's back and legs almost shaved, with thick ruffs around the neck and knees. Instead, Sunshine's coat was shaggy, a lot like a lamb, in fact. Mandy knew that poodles had a special kind of coat that didn't shed hair like other dogs did, which made them popular with people who had allergies or who didn't like sweeping up dog hair around their homes.

"Are you ready, James?" Mandy said. "Let's go outside and take some pictures of her."

"Ready," he said, wolfing down the last mouthful of scone. He carried his plate over to Dr. Emily and thanked her again. Then he picked up his digital camera and followed Mandy out of the kitchen door.

Sunshine paused to sniff at the fresh air in the garden. Her small nose twitched. Then she ran around joyously in a circle and pushed out her back legs, scraping at the grass one leg at a time. She reminded Mandy even more of a lamb — and then she remembered Frida and Ken and felt her spirits sink.

"Right," James said, dragging her thoughts back to the present, "can you hold her still for me?"

Mandy called Sunshine and instantly the poodle ran to Mandy's side and sat down, looking up as if to say, "Yes?"

"Perfect shot!" James cried.

Sunshine spotted something over in the flower bed and dashed off to investigate. Mandy and James watched her use her front paw to pull out an old, rather deflated soccer ball from the undergrowth. She yapped excitedly and began dribbling it with her nose. She raced after the ball, zigzagging gleefully across the lawn.

Mandy burst out laughing. "Go, Sunshine!" she shouted.

The poodle stopped, seized the ball in her teeth, and shook it hard, then dropped it so it bounced away before setting off after it again at a fast pace. James handed Mandy his camera and blocked her as the little dog hurtled toward him. He crouched, ready to spring.

"I'll tackle you if you try to get past!" he warned playfully.

Sunshine herded the ball toward him, then, at the last moment, she swerved off to James's left. Mandy applauded as the poodle drove the ball hard with her nose, then sat down to watch it roll between two bushes. It thudded to a halt against the garden fence.

"Goal!" Mandy yelled, jumping up and down.

"What a star!" James said admiringly. "She's got real talent. Maybe she belongs to a soccer player."

"I saw that!" said an admiring voice. Mandy turned to see Simon stepping out of the clinic's back door. "What style, Sunshine!" he said. "I was watching from the window."

· The poodle was panting but she happily accepted the congratulatory pats of her three admirers.

"Isn't she amazing?" Mandy said, giving James his camera. "Let's go inside. I want to give her a bowl of water."

They took Sunshine into the small kitchen in the clinic. She drank deeply, then wolfed down a bowl of dry food. Mandy carefully measured the amount for a small to medium-sized dog, guessing Sunshine's weight to be about twenty-eight pounds.

Simon was looking thoughtful. "You know," he said, "I'd like to feature Sunshine on my show on Dales Radio." Mandy remembered that Simon, who had always been an amateur radio enthusiast, had just been offered a show on Saturday mornings on the local radio station.

"What do you mean, feature her?" said James, pushing his glasses up on his nose and looking interested.

"I've been hosting a weekly show on topics concerning animals," Simon explained. "If we talked about finding Sunshine on Welford's village green, it would be a way of trying to locate her owner as well as highlighting the issue of losing pets. What do you say, Mandy?"

"Fantastic!" Mandy declared. "Oh, Simon, why didn't I think of it before? Would you really do that?"

"Sure," he said. "It's a great way to reach people who don't live in Welford and haven't had a chance to see the posters. You know, I'm pretty sure — since your mom and dad haven't ever seen Sunshine before — that she probably lives somewhere else."

"Could you ask people to contact Animal Ark if they have any information?" Mandy requested.

"Yes, of course we will," Simon said. "I'll bet we'll get results!"

James grinned. "Sunshine's going to be a radio star!"

"It'll be a golden opportunity," Mandy said. "A chance to reach thousands of people all at once. Someone must know her." She reached out to stroke Sunshine, who had curled into a ball on the rug. Her black nose, smudged with dirt from the yard, rested on her front legs.

"She's tired," James said.

"I'm not surprised," Simon commented. "She ran circles around you playing soccer!"

"I'll take her back to the house," said Mandy.

"Should I start making the flyers?" James offered.

"Yes, please." Mandy nodded. "I'll do some, too. The more we advertise, the luckier we'll be, I'm sure."

But as she said good-bye to James and walked inside with Sunshine dozing in her arms, she couldn't help hoping that Sunshine's owners didn't appear *too* quickly. She was one of the most adorable, affectionate, and fun little dogs Mandy had ever met!

All that evening, Sunshine stayed close to Mandy, following her around the house, upstairs and down. She sat obediently under the table during supper, lying at

Mandy's feet. When she went into the living room to watch television, Sunshine sat beside her chair.

"Isn't she good?" Dr. Emily remarked. "And she's so attached to you, Mandy."

"She has very good taste," Mandy teased, delighted that Sunshine had singled her out for special affection.

"I just called the hospital," Dr. Adam said, skirting Sunshine as he approached his favorite armchair. "Ken is doing well, though he keeps asking about Tess and the sheep."

"One of us will go up to Syke Farm again tomorrow," Dr. Emily said. "Then we can give him a firsthand report on how things are going."

Mandy yawned. "I'd like to go, too. I want to see Tess and Frida."

"Of course," said her father. "Now, how about getting an early night? You look sleepy."

"Yes," Mandy said, suddenly looking forward to her bed. "Can Sunshine . . . ?"

"Sleep in the kitchen?" Dr. Emily smiled. "Yes, of course. I'll get a spare basket from the residential unit for you. It'll be warm on the floor by the heating vent."

Mandy had secretly hoped that Sunshine would be allowed to sleep in her bedroom. But she didn't say anything because her parents were already breaking the rules by letting Sunshine stay in their house rather than

the residential unit. Instead, she took the poodle outside for a last, brief walk in the yard.

Dr. Emily had found a basket that was the perfect
size for Sunshine. A thick, gray blanket had been folded
inside it.

"Here," Mandy said, showing Sunshine. The dog got
into it and lay down. "Good girl," Mandy told her. She
kissed her on the top of her head. "Sleep well. I won't be
far away. Just upstairs." Mandy switched off the light
and shut the door firmly.

She started up the stairs. Halfway up, she heard a
scraping and thumping noise. She paused to listen.
There was a sudden pattering of paws on carpet.
Sunshine had raced up the stairs behind her!

"Sunshine! How did you get out?" Mandy petted the
poodle, who whimpered and licked her hand. "I'm sorry.
You have to go back to your own bed." She carried
Sunshine back to the kitchen and settled her in the basket once more.

"Stay!" Mandy ordered. Then she closed the door and
dragged a straight-backed wooden chair up against it
for good measure. On the other side, Sunshine whined.

"Good girl," Mandy called, feeling sorry for her. "Stay
there now!"

She had just reached her bedroom when there was a
clatter and a thump. Sunshine appeared a moment

later, out of breath. She greeted Mandy as if she hadn't seen her in ages. Her tail was wagging furiously and her bright little button eyes were fixed lovingly on Mandy's face.

"You're a true escape artist!" Mandy picked her up and hugged her. "But you can't sleep with me!"

For a third time, she took the poodle back to the kitchen. The chair had toppled over and was lying on its side in the hallway.

"Is everything OK?" Dr. Emily called from the living room.

"Fine, Mom," Mandy called back. She didn't want to risk Sunshine being sent to the residential unit. Sunshine looked crestfallen. She lowered her gaze and put her chin on her paws in the basket. The blanket engulfed her body. She looked more like a little peach-colored cloud than ever, Mandy thought.

"Sweet girl . . . stay!" She tried to be really commanding. Sunshine cocked her head as Mandy shut the door. She picked up the chair and, this time, wedged the back of it under the door handle. Then she ran upstairs to bed.

She was just drifting off to sleep, thinking about Ken Hudson, Frida, and Tess, when she heard a loud crash. She waited, holding her breath.

"It can't be . . ." she muttered to herself in the darkness. But it was. In came Sunshine, flying up the stairs in search of Mandy and leaping straight into her bed. Mandy dissolved into helpless giggles as she had her face washed by Sunshine's soft tongue.

"You're impossible!" she whispered lovingly. "Now be quiet and go to sleep." She held her breath for a moment, waiting to see if her parents were coming upstairs to investigate. But all was quiet. Mandy decided that Sunshine had made it perfectly clear where she wanted to spend the night, and she wasn't causing any harm by sharing her bed, was she?

Sunshine curled up in a tight ball on top of the comforter and gave a sigh of pure contentment. That settled it; there was no way Mandy could take her back downstairs. Within moments, the little dog was deeply asleep, a warm, gently breathing bundle pressed against Mandy's legs.

Five

Mandy was awakened by something that felt like a warm, wet washcloth dabbing at her ear. The alarm clock rang shrilly in the background. She opened her eyes with a start, reaching with one hand to turn off her alarm clock while she fended off Sunshine with the other. The poodle's small, pink tongue found Mandy's earlobe, then her cheek. Then she began to paw at Mandy's arm.

"Didn't I wake up quickly enough?" Mandy laughed. "Hi, Sunshine." The poodle wagged her tail, shook her curly little body, then jumped off the bed. She sat down and looked expectantly at Mandy, cocking her head as if to say, "Come on, sleepyhead!"

Mandy stretched. "It's Saturday," she announced to the dog. "The day of our radio interview. You need to have a bath so you'll look your best for the people at the radio station."

She got out of bed and found her clothes. Sunshine followed her to the bathroom and waited outside the door while she washed and dressed. Opening the door, Mandy kneeled down and gathered the poodle into her arms to hug her.

"You are *so* sweet," she told her. "You watch over me like an angel. I hope you're not worried. We're going to find your owner, I promise. Meanwhile, you can stay here and I'll take good care of you."

In the kitchen, Dr. Adam and Dr. Emily were reading the morning newspapers. A big brown pot of tea was on the table between them.

"Sleep well, you two?" Dr. Emily smiled. "I picked up the chair Sunshine knocked over. I guessed she was in with you."

"She was so good, Mom," Mandy said, pulling a box of cereal from the cupboard. "She hardly moved until my alarm went off. It was clever of her to escape from the kitchen like that."

"Hmm," said Dr. Adam, "she really doesn't like to be locked up alone, does she?"

Mandy agreed. Sunshine was far happier when she had company, it was true.

"I'd take her outside for a little bit," Dr. Emily advised.

"Oh, yes," Mandy said. She opened the door, and Sunshine obediently trotted out. Mandy waited, watching her stretch and sniff around on the grass. The sky was a soft blue. It wasn't warm yet, but it was going to be another lovely day.

"*Brrr*," Mandy's father said. "Bring her in now, sweetie. It's chilly with that door open."

"Sunshine!" Mandy called. In she came, dew on her paws, her tail wagging. She sat beside Mandy's chair at the table and looked up while Mandy opened a new box of cereal: bran flakes with dried blueberries. It came out of the box in a rush, overfilling her breakfast bowl and raining down on Sunshine's head like petals from a flower.

"Oops!" Mandy said. "Sorry, Sunshine." The poodle pounced on the scattered blueberries, licking them up one by one, carefully avoiding the bran flakes. Mandy chuckled. "I've never seen a dog eat berries before!"

"Neither have I," said Dr. Emily, smiling down at Sunshine.

Mandy found a dustpan and brush and cleaned up the bran flakes, which Sunshine clearly didn't like.

"Do you want to go with me to Syke Farm later?" her dad asked.

"Yes, please," Mandy said. "And can you or Mom drive me and James over to the radio station in Walton this morning?"

"I can," Dr. Emily answered. "Come and find me in the clinic when you're ready to go."

Mandy began to eat her cereal. "OK." Her mouth full, she waved as her parents went off in separate directions: her father upstairs, her mother next door. Then James arrived at the back door. He knocked three times, grinning at Mandy through the window in the top half of the door.

To Mandy's surprise, Sunshine gave a frantic, high-pitched bark and began spinning around until Mandy thought she was going to collapse from dizziness. She rushed to open the door.

James stood there, looking surprised. Sunshine saw him and stopped. Panting, she sat down, looking satisfied with herself.

"Wow!" James exclaimed.

"I don't know what that was all about!" Mandy said.

James came over and looked at her cereal bowl. "Eat up," he advised. "We've got to get Sunshine ready."

"I haven't had much of a chance this morning!" Mandy protested. She began to spoon up her bran flakes and tell James about Sunshine's fondness for blueberries.

"That's a pretty strange snack for a dog. I know Blackie won't eat fruit," he said. "Of course, it's the sort of health food a soccer player might eat. Hey, do you think Sunshine belongs to someone really famous?" He gazed down at her with new respect. "I could get to meet a professional player!" Then he pulled out some neatly folded flyers from his jacket pocket and put them on the table. "Here, I made these."

Mandy opened them out. Sunshine's adorable face looked back at her. James had outlined her photograph in black ink and typed a paragraph about her under the heading:

DO YOU KNOW THIS DOG?

FOUND ON WELFORD'S VILLAGE GREEN ON FRIDAY MORNING, A MEDIUM-SIZED APRICOT MINIATURE POODLE. VERY WELL-BEHAVED AND SWEET-NATURED.

PLEASE CONTACT ANIMAL ARK VETERINARY CLINIC IF YOU HAVE ANY INFORMATION THAT MIGHT HELP HER TO FIND HER OWNER.

"That's great, James!" she said.

"Finished?" he urged, pointing at her bowl.

Mandy took a last mouthful. She nodded. "Dad and I are going up to Syke Farm later, to see how Jack Spiller is doing. Want to come?"

"Definitely," he began, then added, "no, wait, I can't. I promised to help my dad paint the garage."

"Oh," said Mandy, disappointed.

"Well, anyway," James went on, rolling up his sleeves, "let's get going. We've got to get Sunshine ready for her big day!"

Sunshine sat at the bathroom door as Mandy began running warm water into the bathtub. James had gone in search of some old towels. Mandy picked up the special animal shampoo and opened the cap. It smelled of herbs and a gentle antiflea treatment.

"You can bring her in now," she said as James came back.

James picked her up and carried her over to the bathtub. Sunshine's front legs began to paddle and Mandy burst out laughing. "Oh, look, James, she's swimming!"

James lowered Sunshine gently into the water and scooped handfuls of it over her back, wetting her thoroughly.

"Good girl," Mandy praised her as she quickly

massaged in the shampoo. It frothed around her neck and Sunshine sneezed and shook herself vigorously. Bubbles flew everywhere. Mandy rinsed her using a plastic jug, and then let the water run out of her fur, squeezing the excess from the damp woolly coat with her hands.

"She looks like a sheep that's just been shorn," James remarked.

Wrapped in a towel, Sunshine began to shiver with cold. Mandy rubbed her dry, then hurried downstairs and let her onto the grass outside. The little dog ran around in circles, rolling onto her back and paddling her legs in the air. When most of the water had evaporated from her coat, Mandy took her back upstairs and brushed her until she was as smooth and fluffy as a cloud.

"She likes this part," observed James, watching.

Sunshine sat still, allowing Mandy to brush her tail and her ears. She lay on her back and dozed while Mandy brushed her tummy and under each front leg. Mandy fluffed up the topknot of curls on her head — and the job was done.

"You look perfect," she told the poodle. She kissed Sunshine on the nose. "And you smell good, too!"

Dr. Emily parked the car outside a squat, redbrick building in Walton. "Here we are," she said.

Mandy slipped a collar and leash over Sunshine's fluffy head and they all got out of the car. "Best behavior," she whispered to the poodle as they stepped inside. Sunshine wagged her tail, greeting the young woman at a front desk.

"Hello," said Dr. Emily. "I'm Dr. Emily Hope and this is my daughter, Mandy, and her friend James Hunter. We're here to be interviewed by Simon —"

"Yes," the receptionist broke in, nodding enthusiastically. "We're expecting you! This must be Sunshine, the lost poodle?" She bent to pet her. "Aren't you a doll? OK, come this way, please."

James and Mandy, Dr. Emily and Sunshine were led up a flight of stairs to a small room where Simon was sitting at a table.

"Aha!" he said, grinning. "Hi, guys! Welcome to Radio Dales!" He stood up, and the wooden chair he was sitting on toppled backward and fell to the floor with a startling clatter. Sunshine yapped, then began to turn in circles, barking loudly.

Mandy crouched down and held her still. "Sunshine, hush!" The poodle let herself be soothed. "She does this whenever she hears loud noises," Mandy explained. "They really make her nervous. Maybe something happened to scare her when she was a puppy."

"Well, she doesn't look nervous now," Simon said, picking up his chair. Sure enough, Sunshine was watching him with her ears pricked, her tail beating softly against Mandy's arm.

"Which of you am I going to interview? How about you, Mandy?" Simon chuckled. "Or should I begin with Sunshine?"

Mandy suddenly felt a little shy. She smiled at Simon. "Me, I guess," she said, and swallowed hard.

"Good. I'll show you around before we start, if you want," he suggested. He glanced at his watch. "We go on the air at eleven and it's ten-fifteen now. There's time for a tour."

"Yes, please," James said. "I've never been at a radio station before."

Simon led them along a windowless corridor and pointed out mixing rooms, where prerecorded pieces were put together; a relaxation room where a couple of DJs were leafing through a huge stack of news-papers; and a row of closed doors with red lights above them, which led into studios. A glowing red light meant there was a program on the air right at that moment, Simon explained, so those rooms were strictly off-limits!

"This is the studio that really matters," Simon told them

after the tour, herding them through a door with a red light outside on the wall above it. "This is *my* studio!"

Mandy looked around the small room. It had sound-proofing on all four walls — square, spongy-looking tiles with little holes in them — and through a rectangular window she could see a bank of computers and several telephones. A man wearing headphones sat at a desk.

"That's our sound engineer, Gary," Simon said, waving. Gary waved back.

"Now, Mandy, you sit across from me at this table. You'll speak into this microphone, OK?"

Mandy looked at the two suspended microphones, one on each side of the table, and her heart began to do nervous little flip-flops.

"Just talk normally," Simon was saying, "and keep looking at me so it feels like we're having a conversation with no one else listening. And try not to cough because you'll deafen our listeners! When you see the red light come on, you'll know we're on the air, OK?"

Mandy nodded and sat down. Simon adjusted the microphone until it hung level with her mouth and handed her a pair of headphones. When Mandy put them on, Sunshine gave her a curious look and lay down on her feet. Mandy felt very nervous and wondered if Sunshine could sense it.

"Good luck," James mouthed, as Simon pointed to a couple of chairs against the far wall.

"Should I take Sunshine?" Dr. Emily offered. She tugged at the leash, but Sunshine tugged back, staying where she was.

"Can she stay with me?" Mandy asked Simon.

"Of course!" he said. "This is a live show, so if she barks or sneezes or something, it'll make it all the more authentic."

Wearing the cumbersome headphones, Mandy kept an eye on the clock as it inched toward eleven. Behind the glass window, Gary made hand signals to Simon as he counted down the seconds until the live broadcast; then he cued the program's familiar theme tune, which played into the headphones. Mandy's heart began to pound.

"Relax." Simon smiled, looking very professional and at ease. "I'll ask you to explain how you found Sunshine and a few other details. Just talk as though we were in the kitchen at Animal Ark, OK?"

"OK," Mandy said, taking a deep breath. "I'm ready."

Simon looked up at Gary for a signal and flipped a couple of buttons on the equipment in front of him. Mandy's microphone light went on.

"It's a beautiful morning here in Walton, and Radio Dales is delighted to welcome Mandy Hope, from the

Animal Ark Veterinary Clinic in Welford, to the studio, along with a lost dog she calls Sunshine. Hello, Mandy," Simon said. He was speaking in his normal voice, smiling to make it sound warm and friendly.

Mandy felt her face flush. "Hello," she said. Her voice echoed back at her through the headphones, sounding strange. She half turned and made a face at her mother and James, who gave her a thumbs-up sign.

"Would you like to tell us a little bit about this poodle?" Simon prompted.

"I found her on Welford's village green yesterday morning," Mandy began. "She's a very pretty apricot miniature poodle. She wasn't wearing a collar and she doesn't have an identity microchip."

Simon smiled at her encouragingly; she was doing well. "What else can you tell our listeners about Sunshine?"

"She has a very sweet nature," Mandy said, relaxing as her hand reached under the desk and found the top of Sunshine's soft head. It was so easy to talk about the gorgeous little dog that she forgot to feel nervous about being on the radio. "She's also very obedient and affectionate. She's so loving and so good, she must have come from a family who loved her very much."

"I can vouch for Sunshine," Simon told his audience. "She's in the studio right now — a beautiful little dog — and good as gold, too. So if anyone knows anything about Sunshine, please get in touch with someone at Animal Ark. Mandy and Sunshine will be very grateful."

He signaled to Mandy to be quiet while he gave out the phone number of the clinic, then announced the name of the song he was about to play. Suddenly, Mandy's microphone light went out — and it was all over.

"That was great!" Simon said.

"Thanks, Simon." Mandy smiled, standing up. "I hope we get some calls."

"I'm sure we will," Dr. Emily said, coming over and giving Mandy a hug.

After lunch, Mandy settled Sunshine in her basket in the kitchen and gave her a dog treat. Dr. Emily was doing some paperwork at the kitchen table.

"She'll be fine with me," she said. "Off you go, and say hello to Jack Spiller for me."

"I will," Mandy said, backing out of the door. Sunshine cocked her head, watching, but made no attempt to follow her. Mandy could hear her father starting the Land Rover, so she ran to the parking lot and jumped in. On the way up to Syke Farm, she filled him in on all the details of her visit to the radio station.

"It sounds like you were very professional. Good for you," her father said.

"I *want* to find her owner," Mandy said. "But, at the same time, I really don't want her to go."

Her dad patted her knee as he pulled up at the farm. "I know, sweetheart," he said. "It's going to be hard to say good-bye. Hey, look, there's Jack." He waved a hand out of the window.

"Adam! Mandy!" Mr. Spiller strode forward, smiling.

He was tall and dark-haired and wore a dark green waterproof coat over faded jeans tucked into green rubber boots. "How are you?"

"Fine," Dr. Adam said. "How's everything here?"

"Busy!" Jack said, taking off his cap and wiping the back of his hand across his brow. "We've had another multiple birth and two more singles, born this morning around dawn."

"All doing well?" Dr. Adam checked.

"All fine," answered the farmer.

"Can I go and find Tess and see the lambs?" asked Mandy.

"Sure," Jack Spiller said. "Some of the lambs have been turned out into the field. The new ones are in the barn. I haven't seen the dog much today — she's making herself scarce."

Mandy walked to the field and stood at the gate. Spring grass had turned the landscape the color of mint. The ewes grazed contentedly, plucking at the sweet, new shoots, while around them the lambs tried out their wobbly legs. They sprang around like windup toys, gleeful and bouncing.

Mandy went in search of Tess. The sheepdog was lying in the shadow of a tree, her chin on her front paws. Mandy called to her, but Tess didn't move. Her tail was still and, as she approached the sheepdog, Mandy saw the deepest look of bewilderment and misery in her dark brown eyes.

"Oh, Tess," she said, smoothing her soft head. "You miss Ken, I know."

Tess just whimpered and turned her head away. Mandy had an idea. She hurried back to her father.

"If there's anything I can do, Jack," he was saying to Jack Spiller, "just give me a call."

"Thanks so much, Adam," he answered.

"Dad!" Mandy said. "Can we take Tess to see Ken? Please?"

"Tess is pining," Jack Spiller said. "Poor dog. Doesn't seem to want to eat a thing. I found her food bowl still full this morning. She hasn't touched it."

Dr. Adam looked at Mandy's pleading face. "OK," he replied. "But I don't think Marion is going to be thrilled."

"She won't mind," Mandy insisted. "I'll keep Tess in the garden outside Ken's window."

"I'll get going, then," Jack Spiller said. "I'll give you a call if I need you. Thanks again."

"Bye, Mr. Spiller," Mandy called. She'd opened the trunk of the Land Rover. "Come, Tess! Up!"

The sheepdog's ears shot up and she leaped into the rear of the car. She looked around shiftily, unsure of where she was being taken, but Mandy soothed her and she sat down. "Stay, girl," she said softly. Tess crouched and waited for further instructions.

"She's an excellent working dog," Dr. Adam remarked, getting in behind the wheel. "High-strung, but a good, loyal dog."

"She misses Ken really bad," Mandy said. "I'm so glad that she'll have a chance to see him. It will reassure her."

"Don't be too long at the hospital, OK?" Dr. Adam said, accelerating away from the farm. "I've got a busy afternoon. You take Tess to Ken's window and I'll make some calls in the car."

"OK," said Mandy. "Too bad it's so busy. I wanted to spend some more time with the lambs."

"I know," said her father. "There'll be other chances this week, I'm sure."

By the time they reached the hospital parking lot, Mandy could hear Tess's nervous breathing. She was excited, eager to give the lovely dog a treat by seeing her owner. She got out and opened the trunk to fasten a leash to Tess's collar.

"Come, Tess!" she said.

Tess jumped out and kept pace, walking to heel as Mandy led her around the side of the building into the small courtyard garden. A door opened suddenly and a man wheeled a metal cart down a ramp toward a waiting van. It was piled high with used hospital linens. Mandy raised her hand in a casual wave.

"Lovely day!" he said. He didn't even seem to notice Tess, so Mandy walked on confidently until she located Ken's window; it was the one that directly faced the only tree in the garden. He was sitting in a chair with his feet on a stool, reading a book. Mandy thought he looked a little better already.

She tapped gently on the window. Ken lowered his book and looked out. He stood up, and Tess spotted him at once. Her silky ears shot up. Her tail wagged hesitantly, then she went right up to the window and pressed her nose against the glass.

Ken waved and smiled.

"How are you?" Mandy mouthed, but Ken didn't see her because his eyes were on his dog. He struggled with a tight latch on the frame and finally, the window swung open.

Ken reached a hand out to Tess. "How's my girl?" he said.

Tess put her front paws on the window, making Ken laugh. Her tail was wagging like crazy and Mandy was struggling to hold on to her. Tess began to whine and squirm. She pulled left and right, then reared up on her hind legs. The claws on her front paws tapped at the glass. Mandy tugged hard at the leash but Tess was determined to try to get inside.

"Steady, there!" Ken told the dog.

"OK!" Mandy puffed. "Tess, you win. Come on, I'll sneak you in that door at the side and you can say a quick hello. We're coming around, Mr. Hudson," she said.

Mandy raced out of the courtyard. The van that had backed up to the door was gone. She opened it and looked around. There was nobody around, so she quickly led Tess down the corridor, toward Ken's room. But once inside the hospital, Tess's tail drooped nervously. She slowed down, her nose quivering at the unfamiliar smells, and her feet scrabbled on the shiny linoleum floor.

"In here!" Mandy hissed, opening the door to Ken's room.

Ken's arms were outstretched to welcome Tess as she came in. She swirled around his legs, looking up at him, her tongue lolling. But she seemed very nervous. Her eyes shifted around and she lay down, then stood up again almost at once.

Ken smoothed Tess's soft head. "Oh, it's great to see you again, girl." He looked at Mandy. "But she's unsure of herself in here, Mandy. Better take her out, OK? It was nice of you to have brought her to me, but I can tell she doesn't think much of hospitals!"

"You'll be home soon, anyway. You look much better," Mandy said. "I'll take her out before someone comes, then. Bye!"

Tess seemed only too happy to be leaving the sterile, shiny ward with its strange smells. She was relieved to be out in the fresh air again. Her tail went up and so did her ears. Mandy set off at a run, heading back to the parking lot. As she rounded the corner, she almost collided with Marion, the head nurse.

"Oh! Careful!" Marion gasped. "Mandy Hope, you gave me a scare!"

"I'm so sorry, Marion," Mandy said, pulling Tess up short. "I was just giving Mr. Hudson's dog a . . ."

Marion interrupted her. "Yes, well, I know it's a shame that we can't allow people to have their pets visit when they're in the hospital, but rules are rules. Not every dog is as beautifully behaved as Twinkle. Now, there was a gentle, sociable animal!"

"I understand," Mandy said. "Well, I'd better get Tess back to Syke Farm. My dad's got a busy afternoon. Bye, Marion."

As she hurried with Tess toward the car, Mandy felt glad that she had taken a chance and brought Tess together with Ken, brief though it was. She hadn't had to tell any lies, but she was relieved just the same that Marion hadn't questioned her too closely.

As Mandy opened the door for Tess, she just hoped the sheepdog knew that her master hadn't deserted her, that he wasn't very far away — and that he would be coming home to her soon.

Six

When Mandy arrived back at Animal Ark, she found James in the kitchen, playing with Sunshine and Blackie.

"Your mom let me in," he told her. "She said you wouldn't be long."

Mandy crouched down to hug Sunshine. Blackie came over and put his muzzle on her leg. "Hello, Blackie," Mandy said. "Dad and I took Tess to see Ken in the hospital," she explained to James. "Tess didn't like it much. She just had a quick hello and then we drove her back to the farm."

She sat down with Sunshine beside her. The little dog didn't make a fuss, or thump her tail on the floor, or even put up a paw to remind Mandy she was there as Blackie sometimes did. She just looked on with her calm, gentle eyes.

"Look at her, James," Mandy said, stroking the poodle. "She's so sweet. She's not . . . *needy* like some dogs are."

"She has a great temperament," James agreed, putting his own hand out to Blackie. "Except when there's a loud noise. Then she's not so good!"

"Sunshine would be the perfect dog to take into the hospital, don't you think?" Mandy said. "Remember how much the patients loved having Twinkle visit them?"

"Yes," James said. "Twinkle seemed to lift everyone's spirits."

"Sunshine would do the same," Mandy continued. She felt suddenly fired up about the idea. "I'm sure people miss their pets so much when they have to stay in a hospital, just like Ken misses Tess. We should take Sunshine to visit the patients!"

"It's a good idea, but we'd have to persuade the head nurse," James said. By now, Blackie was trying to climb onto Mandy's lap, too, so James came over and tugged him away, laughing.

"Are you jealous of Sunshine, Blackie? Anyway," he said, "I came to show you the posters. I made a change — look!"

He had added a single line in a bold script: SUNSHINE'S STORY — AS HEARD ON DALES RADIO!

Mandy smiled. "She's famous — or she soon will be!" she said. "Thanks for doing the posters, James. They're great. Let's go and put a few up."

"Yes," he said, "the sooner we stick them up, the sooner we'll find Sunshine's owners. That's why I've been waiting for you." He fished Blackie's leash out of his pocket. The Labrador bounded over to him, tail wagging expectantly.

Mandy put Sunshine down and found her leash. She grabbed an apple from the fruit bowl as she passed it and opened the door to the yard. Sunshine stood on the threshold and sniffed the air. She looked around carefully before stepping outside, her tail wagging.

"Funny little girl," Mandy said affectionately.

Blackie pranced around, his big, black paws getting in Sunshine's way.

"Sunshine isn't impressed," James told the Labrador. "She's too much of a lady for you!"

Blackie seemed determined to get Sunshine to play with him as they walked along, but the poodle stayed firmly at Mandy's heels. She refused his attention —

just as Blackie refused James's commands to leave her alone.

As they approached the village green, Mandy saw Walter Pickard on his knees, wielding a small trowel. "Uh-oh," she said. "Walter's repairing the pansy bed."

"He won't be very pleased to see Sunshine, then," James said.

Mandy noticed that Sara Hardy, who ran the village restaurant with her husband, had been admiring Walter's gardening. She spotted Mandy and came over.

"Nice weather for a school break, isn't it?" Sara greeted them. "John's on a camping trip in the south of France, lucky thing. Oh, who's this?" She looked down at Sunshine, who was sitting on Mandy's foot.

"Hi, Sara," Mandy replied. "This is Sunshine. We're looking for her owners."

"The apricot poodle, of course!" she said. "I heard about her on the radio. Have you had any response?"

"Not so far," James admitted. He handed Sara one of his flyers. "Could you please put this up in the Fox and Goose for us?"

"Do you have more than one? I'm on my way to the post office, then the bank. I'll put a couple up there, too, if you want." Sara had bent down to ruffle Sunshine's woolly head, and Blackie craned over to snuffle in her ear for some attention.

Sara laughed. James hauled him away. "That would be great. Thanks," he said.

"Thanks, Sara," Mandy said gratefully. "Bye."

"Good luck!" she called.

They walked on. James handed a flyer to a man carrying a sack of potatoes. "Sunshine?" the man read out loud, frowning. "I recognize the name of the dog. . . ."

"Yes," Mandy said, "she's a radio star! Maybe you heard about her on Dales Radio?"

"Oh, yes!" he said. He smiled down at Sunshine. "She's a good-looking little dog. Someone will claim her, I'm sure. I wish you luck."

"Thank you," James said.

It was warm and Sunshine's small pink tongue peeped out as she panted.

"Let's go back," Mandy suggested. "Sunshine and I need something to drink."

"Well, we're just about out of posters, anyway," James said. He pushed his hair out of his eyes.

"Give the rest to me and I'll put them up in the reception area at Animal Ark," Mandy said. "Let's take Sunshine to the hospital tomorrow! If you print off a few more tonight, we can hand them out to people while we're there. They'll come from a larger area than just Welford so they might recognize her from their neighborhood."

"Good idea," James said. "OK, I'll see you tomorrow."

"See you," Mandy said.

That evening during dinner at Animal Ark, Sunshine seemed even more nervous than usual. The telephone rang twice, and each time it trilled Sunshine began turning in circles, barking. The second time, she jumped up into Mandy's lap and pushed her cold, wet nose under Mandy's chin.

"She's frightened of the telephone!" Mandy decided, mopping up milk that had splashed onto her knee from her glass. She stroked Sunshine, calming her, and put her on the floor.

Her mother looked down at the poodle under the table. "I know where *you'll* be spending the night tonight!" she said.

"She hates to be left alone, Mom," Mandy said. "She's really scared."

"I know," Dr. Emily said. "Just don't get too attached to her. She's a great dog, but she belongs to somebody else who loves her even more. Remember that."

"I'll remember," Mandy said, and put a hand down to the soft cloud-coat pressing against her leg. She could only imagine how sad Sunshine's owner must feel, wondering what had become of the adorable poodle. But saying good-bye to Sunshine was not going to be easy!

Sunshine slept peacefully at the foot of Mandy's bed. She loved the weight and the warmth of the poodle against her feet. Once or twice during the night, Mandy woke up and put out a hand, making contact with the poodle's curls, and received a small, reassuring lick in return.

When the alarm clock chimed, Sunshine was startled awake at once, barking crazily. She jumped off the bed and turned in her tight little circles until Mandy shut off the clock.

"Silly goose!" she chuckled. "It's only a clock! It won't hurt you."

She dressed and took Sunshine into the yard, then fed her and gave her a bowl of milk. Her father was singing tunelessly in the kitchen, making Sunday morning pancakes. James arrived just as a steaming stack of freshly made pancakes had been placed on the kitchen table. His eyes lit up.

"Morning," Mandy said, stifling a yawn. "Pancake?"

"Hmm, yes, please," said James.

Mandy stood up and got the syrup. "Will you drive us over to Walton Hospital this morning, Dad?" she asked.

Dr. Adam plunged the frying pan under the cold tap and it sizzled. "Mom will take you, sweetie. I'm going out on calls this morning."

"Yes, I'll be happy to take you." Dr. Emily appeared, still in her robe. "I'd like to see Ken. I've got a fruit basket for him. Hi, James!"

Sunshine sat close to Mandy under the table while they had breakfast. Mandy slipped her a dried blueberry and felt the gentle beat of Sunshine's tail against her calf. She really was an amazing little dog!

It was raining lightly when they set off for Walton. James sat in the backseat with Sunshine, who kept her eyes fixed loyally on Mandy in the front. Mandy held the basket of fruit on her lap.

"You don't exactly have Marion's *permission* to take Sunshine into the ward, do you, Mandy?" Dr. Emily pointed out.

"I want her to meet Sunshine first," Mandy explained. "That will help her make up her mind, I'm sure."

Marion had just arrived for her shift when Dr. Emily drew into the parking lot. Mandy jumped out, with Sunshine on her leash. Marion was locking the door of her car as Mandy came up, followed by James.

"Hello, Marion," she said.

"Good morning, Mandy, and hello there, James!" Marion looked over at the Land Rover and raised a hand. "Hello, Emily!"

"This is Sunshine," Mandy said, feeling proud. The

poodle sat down at her feet and looked up at Marion, cocking her head.

"Hello, Sunshine," said Marion. "What a pretty little dog! Is she yours?"

Mandy shook her head. "No, she's lost and we've taken her in while we try to find her owners. Do you think I could take her inside, please? She's so good and very gentle. I really think the patients will love her."

Marion folded her arms and looked down at Sunshine, who stood up and wagged her tail. Then she looked at Mandy and at James. Dr. Emily came over and stood, watching from a short distance away.

"I'm here to see Ken!" Dr. Emily explained. "But I can vouch for Sunshine — she's immaculately behaved and, as a breed, poodles don't shed their coats, either. So, no dog hair in the wards."

"Very well, then!" said Marion, her blue eyes twinkling. "Bring her in. We've got plenty of patients who need cheering up. But the first sign of trouble and she'll be outside before you can say 'poodle'!"

There was a dayroom on the ground floor of the hospital, a communal sitting room for recovering patients. Mandy took Sunshine in on her leash and immediately there was a chorus of delighted "aahs"! A little girl with her leg in a brace reached out with one hand, her eyes wide. Mandy led Sunshine toward her.

"Does she bite?" the girl asked.

"No," Mandy said. "You can pet her if you want."

Sunshine wagged her tail as the girl laid her hand on the little dog's head. "She's nice!" she said.

Marion kept a beady eye on the poodle, stopping her patients when they encouraged Sunshine to jump into their laps. "None of that," she said. "And Clara, you'll have to *wash* that hand now!"

But Mandy could tell she was delighted with the effect Sunshine was having. Even patients who hadn't seemed very friendly at first were soon smiling, laughing, and reaching out to the poodle. Sunshine seemed to enjoy the hour she spent doing the rounds of the room, spending time with each person in turn. Mandy was so proud of the pretty dog. She was affectionate without being boisterous, accepting pats and strokes from a crowd of strangers. Her little tail kept wagging.

By the time they had walked up and down three of the wards, stopping by the bedsides of those who wanted to meet the dog, Mandy felt that Sunshine had more than done her duty. "Should we take her to meet Ken?" she suggested.

James agreed. He had happily answered endless questions about Sunshine, who, it turned out, was really quite well known because many of the patients had heard Mandy being interviewed on the radio.

"What a wonderful dog!" Marion exclaimed as she hurried past, her heels tapping along the corridor. "So well trained!"

James knocked on Ken Hudson's door.

"Come in!" called Ken. His voice seemed stronger already.

Mandy led Sunshine in. Dr. Emily was sitting beside Ken, who was in the chair by the window. He was wearing a new plaid robe and his hair was neatly brushed. There was healthy color in his cheeks, and his eyes were twinkling again. A bowl sat on the table beside him, overflowing with grapes, bananas, and apples.

"Hello!" said Mandy.

"We brought Sunshine to meet you," James told him.

"Ah! The famous poodle," said Ken. "Your mom was just telling me all about her."

Sunshine went up to the chair and stood on her hind legs. She licked Ken's hand and wagged her whole body. Mandy tugged her back just as she was preparing to jump into his lap. She could tell that Ken was taken aback by the small, friendly dog. He was used to working dogs, who were more reserved.

"Very good," he said, looking a little uncomfortable. "You're keeping an eye on my Tess for me, aren't you, Mandy?"

"Yes, I am," Mandy promised. "Tess misses you, but she's doing fine."

Dr. Emily stood up. "It's time to go," she said. "Take care, Ken."

"I will," he said. "I'll be out of here soon. And thank you for the fruit."

On the way back to the car Mandy let Sunshine off her leash and allowed her to run around on a patch of the hospital's lawn. Sunshine rolled luxuriously on her back, rubbing her cheeks along the sun-drenched grass. "You deserve this," Mandy told her. "What a good girl you've been!"

As the poodle wagged her tail and came over to Mandy's side, she thought about Sunshine's owner. Someone somewhere must be heartbroken about Sunshine's disappearance. But why hadn't they tried to find her?

Sunshine seemed delighted to be back at Animal Ark. She ran around in the kitchen, rubbed her nose on Mandy's dad's hand, then sat at the door to the yard, asking to go out. Mandy stood and watched her from the doorway, listening with one ear to what her father was saying.

". . . so I think it's good news. Very good news!"

"What is?" Mandy said. She looked at her father, then at James, who was openmouthed.

"You're not listening!" James accused her.

"Mandy," her father repeated, "I said I had a phone call from Sunshine's owner. A Mr. Lex. He says the dog's name is Peachy and he's coming over tomorrow morning."

"What?" Mandy cried. "Oh, my *goodness*! Tomorrow morning? But it's too soon! How am I going to . . . ?" She trailed off, feeling a pang of sadness. It was good news for Sunshine — that was what she had to remember. Sunshine would be going home! Home, where she belonged.

Her father and James were still looking at her.

"Good," Mandy said flatly. "That's great news." Then she went out into the yard to find the poodle, determined to spend every possible moment with her before her owner arrived to get her.

Seven

When she woke up the following morning, Mandy had a hollow feeling in her tummy. A second later, she remembered why. It was Sunshine's last morning.

"Can I skip breakfast, Mom?" she asked.

Dr. Emily was buttering a slice of toast. She looked up and raised her eyebrows. "Nothing to eat?" she asked Mandy. "Not even a mouthful?"

Mandy shook her head. "Maybe later. Can I take a handful of dried blueberries for Sunshine and play with her outside?"

Dr. Emily nodded. She caught Mandy's hand as she

went by and gave it a little squeeze. "It's a great day for Sunshine, remember," she said. "She'll be going back to where she belongs."

"I know," Mandy said. She managed a smile. "Come on, Sunshine!"

The poodle had slept all night curled up in the crook of Mandy's knees. Once or twice she had woken to the dog's sleepy snuffles and put a hand out to touch her topknot of peach-colored curls. Now she watched as Sunshine raced around on the grass, investigating the scent trails of all the creatures who had visited the yard overnight. Mandy laughed as Sunshine found the soccer ball — and pounced! She shook it in her teeth, then plopped it down and deftly butted it toward Mandy with her nose.

Mandy kicked the ball back toward her. Sunshine caught it, shook it again, then rolled it back to Mandy using the top of her head.

"Good girl!" Mandy laughed, sending the ball back. She hoped that Sunshine's owners would be friendly and lived nearby. It would be great if she could visit Sunshine.

The poodle had the ball in her mouth when suddenly her ears pricked up and she dropped it and began to bark. She ran toward the gate.

"Right," said Mandy, looking at her wristwatch. "This must be them. *Shhh*, Sunshine, don't make so much noise. Let's go and say hello."

Mandy looked over the gate and saw a couple with two children heading for the main entrance to Animal Ark. They had parked their big four-wheel-drive vehicle rather carelessly, backing it up right onto the edge of her mother's daffodil bed. Calling the poodle, Mandy dashed into the house and through the connecting door into the back of the clinic. Sunshine was right behind her. Mandy stopped and peeked through the small pane of glass set high in the door that separated the reception area from the treatment rooms. She saw her father shaking hands with Mr. and Mrs. Lex. The children, a boy and a girl, looked about the same age and height, with matching freckles and coppery hair. Mandy guessed they were about ten years old.

"Yes, they're twins," Mrs. Lex was saying to Dr. Adam as Mandy opened the door. "This is Shaun and this is Toni."

Sunshine shot past Mandy and stood in the middle of the floor, wagging her tail.

"Ah!" said Mr. Lex. "Here's *Peachy*!"

"Hello," Mandy said.

Nobody seemed to hear her. She watched as the children reached out to Sunshine, who licked their hands and made them giggle. Mrs. Lex, wearing very high-heeled boots and a tight pair of pale blue jeans, kneeled down to lift Sunshine into her arms.

"Oof," she said, struggling to stand up. "Have you put on weight?" Sunshine wriggled, her tail wagging. She licked Mrs. Lex's chin, and the woman made a face. As she raised her hand to push Sunshine's nose away, Mandy noticed Mrs. Lex's manicured nails, long and painted fire-engine red.

"You're looking *good*, Peach!" Mr. Lex said.

"This is Mandy," Dr. Adam said, drawing Mandy forward. "She's the one who deserves thanking. She rescued Sunshine . . . Peachy . . . and has been a very attentive surrogate mom."

Mrs. Lex put the poodle down. As she did so, her long gold necklace swung out and looped around the little dog's neck. Mandy sprang forward.

"Oops!" She smiled, bending to dislodge it and set the poodle free.

"Thanks, Mandy," said Mrs. Lex, baring her very white teeth in a smile.

Mandy looked over at the twins. The girl, Toni, was staring at her. She seemed shy.

"Hi," Mandy said. "I've loved taking care of your dog. You must have missed her so much!"

Toni didn't answer. Instead she looked at her mother, who nodded.

"Oh, yes!" Mrs. Lex said. "The children have been *miserable* without Peachy."

"Well," Mandy said, doing her best to be cheerful, "tonight Peachy will be back on your bed, keeping your feet warm, where she belongs."

"Oh, I hope *not*!" Mrs. Lex said sharply, then chuckled and wagged a stern finger at her daughter. "Dogs don't belong on beds. Not in *our* house, anyway. Right, Toni?"

The girl nodded again. She looked around, wide-eyed, at the clinic waiting room. "Do you *live* here?" she asked Mandy.

"Yes," she answered. "Well, not *here* exactly, but next door. My mom and dad are vets."

"You must have lots of pets," said Toni.

The poodle was now sitting on Mandy's sneaker, wagging her tail on the floor. "In a way I do," Mandy said. "I help look after the animals that come here."

Mr. Lex had produced a collar attached to a leash. It was lemon yellow and studded with small fake diamond studs. It looked brand-new.

"Here we are!" he said. "This is for you." He brandished it at the poodle, who cocked her head but didn't move off Mandy's foot. The big, broad-shouldered man came over and bent down to fasten it around the poodle's neck. It was too big, and the little dog lifted her hind leg to scratch at her neck. The collar drooped around her throat.

Mandy felt a twinge of unease. Had Mr. Lex forgotten what size his dog was? She hadn't been lost for that long. "Well," she said, looking at Toni, "you must give me your address and phone number so we can keep in touch."

Shaun, who was reading a poster on the wall about flea-and-tick prevention, turned to look at his mother.

"Actually, we're moving," Mrs. Lex said quickly. "We don't have an address yet."

"Oh, where are you moving to?" Dr. Adam said. "I might be able to recommend a vet for you."

"I guess we'll stick to using our old vet," Mr. Lex said, nodding at his wife.

"What's his name?" Dr. Adam asked. "I might know him. . . ."

They were all distracted by a sharp rapping at the window. Sunshine began running in circles, the lemon-colored leash snaking around her on the floor and the too-big collar flapping around her neck. Then she took hold of the hem of Mandy's jeans and began to tug hard.

"It's OK," Mandy said loudly, above the noise of excited yapping, "it's only James!"

Mr. and Mrs. Lex were staring at the poodle. Mrs. Lex covered her ears with the palms of her hands and frowned at the dog. "Stop that!" she cried. "*Naughty* dog!"

Mandy hurriedly pulled the poodle into her arms. *Something is not right here*, she thought. Sunshine — no, *Peachy* — always ran around in circles when she heard a knock or an alarm clock or a car. Surely her owners knew that? As James came in, Mandy let go of Sunshine and the poodle hurried over to welcome him with a wagging tail.

"Hi," said James, looking past Mandy at the crowd in the waiting room.

"This is James Hunter," said Dr. Adam. "This is the Lex family, James, who own . . . um . . . Peachy."

Mr. Lex was glaring at the poodle. Mandy saw him exchange glances with his wife. Quietly, Mandy slipped the collar off the poodle's neck and handed it to Toni. "It's nice of you to have brought a new collar, but I think it's too big for her, don't you?" she said.

Toni looked at Mandy but she didn't answer.

"Great dog," James commented, smiling at Shaun and Toni. "We loved getting to know her. She's a star with a soccer ball. Do you play much with her?"

"I don't like soccer," Shaun announced. "I like motorcycle racing."

"Well, your dog's got real talent," James said, sounding a little uncertain.

Mandy caught his eye. "Can you help me with something?" she asked. "Right now."

James looked surprised. He pushed his glasses higher up on his nose and followed Mandy through the door into a treatment room.

"What's up?" he whispered.

Mandy's heart had begun to pound with nerves. "James!" she breathed. "Something's not right. I don't think Sunshine belongs to them."

James's eyes stretched very wide. "What? Why?" he hissed.

"It's like they don't know her at all! Why buy a collar that's way too big? And where's her old collar, anyway? Why are they so surprised by the way she behaves, like when she runs around in circles? And they won't have her sleeping on a bed, either! She hates sleeping alone. Nothing . . . *fits*!"

James was quiet for a moment. "That boy doesn't even know that Sunshine loves soccer," he said. "What are we going to do?"

Mandy was very worried. She didn't trust the Lexes. She was not going to part with the poodle until she did. But how could she make sure?

"I know," James said suddenly, still whispering. "You told me that Sunshine loves blueberries, remember?"

Mandy nodded. "Yes, but . . ."

"Bring me a handful of blueberry bran flakes, quick!" James urged her. "I've got an idea."

Mandy rushed through to the kitchen, grabbed the cereal box, and hurried back. James was waiting for her with cupped hands.

"Pour!" he instructed. "They're about to leave."

Mandy shook out a handful of flakes and opened the door into the reception room.

"Well, we'll be off, then," Mrs. Lex was saying, smiling at Dr. Adam. "Thank you again."

"Excuse me," James spoke up. "Before you go, can I just give Peachy a farewell treat?" He opened his hand. Shaun and Toni stared.

"Cereal?" Shaun queried.

"Sure!" said Mr. Lex, smiling broadly. "Peachy just loves her bran flakes. She's always hanging around at breakfast, waiting for them to drop on the ground. She's more used to the ones without berries, though."

James went down on one knee and stretched a hand toward the poodle. Tail wagging, Sunshine sniffed at the crispy pile of flakes, then nosed about until she was able to extract a single blueberry that she chewed with

relish. Then she went back, pushing aside the flakes and looking for a second berry.

Mandy took a deep breath. "I'm sorry, but I don't think Sunshine is your dog."

There was a silence. Mr. and Mrs. Lex stared at her.

"Peachy?" Mr. Lex said. "Sure she is! I'm not surprised you got so attached to her. I understand you don't want to say good-bye, but —"

"Mandy," Dr. Adam interrupted, "what do you mean?"

"I mean," Mandy said, feeling bold and very angry,

"that Mr. and Mrs. Lex don't seem to know Sunshine at all." She turned to face the family. "You know nothing about her! How *could* she be yours?"

"Oh, I see," Mrs. Lex said huffily, folding her arms. "I didn't realize that we'd have to bring Peachy's ID papers when we came to get her!"

"Of course she's ours!" Mr. Lex said impatiently. "Look how great she is with my kids."

"She's great with *anybody's* kids," James said. "She's the happiest, friendliest dog in Yorkshire."

Dr. Adam put an arm around Mandy. She was beginning to quiver with indignation. "Dad, I know I'm right," she whispered.

"Leave it to me to handle this," he whispered back. He raised his voice. "Look, Mr. Lex, would you mind giving me the name of your vet? I'd like to call him to check a few things, if you don't mind?"

"We *do* mind!" Mrs. Lex said.

"Let's just go," Mr. Lex announced. "The dog has been badly spoiled by you — ruined, I'd say. I don't want to have to go to all the trouble of teaching her how to behave all over again." He glared at Sunshine, who was sitting in the middle of the floor, looking up with her little tail wagging happily.

"See, Dan," said Mrs. Lex. "Now I smell like dog — and all for nothing!"

"I *told* you it wouldn't work," Shaun whined as he followed his mother and father out of the door. "Why can't we just buy a dog like normal people?"

"I want a kitten, anyway," said Toni. She was still protesting when the door slammed shut behind her.

Dr. Adam, Mandy, and James stared at the closed door in stunned silence. At last, Mandy found her voice.

"We almost lost her! Sunshine was nearly stolen from under our noses!"

Eight

"Now that's what I call thinking on your feet," said Dr. Adam, stirring sugar into a jug of freshly made lemonade. "Well done, both of you."

"I can't believe it!" Mandy said. "We were *so* close to losing Sunshine to those . . . those . . ." She trailed off, at a loss for words.

"Thieves!" James finished.

Mandy's mom handed a glass to James and one to Mandy, who was sitting cross-legged on the carpet in the living room, with Sunshine curled up in her lap.

"It's hard to understand the way some people think," Dr. Emily said. "Mr. and Mrs. Lex must have liked the

108

description of Sunshine from the radio interview and quickly realized they could become the owners of a pretty, and very well-trained, pedigreed dog without having to pay a penny for her!"

"They were so confident!" Mandy said, still feeling outraged, but pleased that she and James had been able to outsmart the family. She poked a finger at the ice in her lemonade, and Sunshine's nose twitched as she dozed, her chin on Mandy's knee.

"Well, Sunshine is quite famous," James reasoned. "Since that interview, I mean."

"We'll be much more careful from now on," Dr. Adam decided. "We'll demand identification from anyone who shows an interest in Sunshine."

"What sort of identification?" asked James.

Dr. Emily sipped her tea. "A reference from a vet will do as proof, or a pet passport, or even some insurance papers with a current photograph," she explained.

"Yes," Mandy agreed. "And I'm not going to let her out of my sight for a minute until we find her real owner!"

James slurped up the last of his drink. "Let's take Blackie and Sunshine out," he suggested.

"Good idea," said Dr. Emily. "It's a gorgeous day. Why not take your bikes and have a picnic? It will take your mind off this morning's drama. I'll make some sandwiches."

"Perfect!" James said at once. "I'll go get Blackie and my bike, Mandy. OK?"

"OK," she said, smiling.

Mandy's dad came over and laid a gentle hand on Sunshine's head. The poodle opened her eyes and looked up at him. Her tail stirred sleepily.

"You're a good girl," Dr. Adam told her. "Somebody must be missing you very much — and we're going to reunite you. Just see if we don't!"

Blackie was used to running alongside James's bike. He loped along, level with the front wheel, his tongue lolling. The breeze lifted his silky black ears, and Mandy was sure he was smiling. She pedaled carefully, watching to see that Sunshine stayed clear of the wheels of her bicycle. She had looped the poodle's leash around her wrist. The little dog scampered along, keeping pace easily, wagging her tail.

They rode by the village green and Mandy called out a greeting to Ernie Bell and Walter Pickard, who were still working on the pansy bed. The sun was warm and Mandy was looking forward to the bottle of juice in the backpack. Her spirits lifted. Sunshine was safe and that was all that mattered.

At the top of the sloping rise out of the village, they propped their bikes against a low stone wall. Mandy took off the poodle's leash and lifted her into the field. Clearing the wall with a single energetic bound, Blackie almost took James with him! He let the Labrador loose and the dog went streaking away, intent on some exciting scent.

"Let's go toward Monkton Spinney," Mandy suggested. "Come on, Sunshine!"

"I think Blackie is trying to impress Sunshine," James observed, laughing. His dog had stopped to dig, sending up a shower of rich, dark earth with his front paws. Sunshine trotted by, ignoring him. Every few seconds, the poodle paused to turn her head to check that Mandy was following.

"I'm here!" Mandy called to her. "I'm coming."

"And I'm starving," James said. "Here's a good place to stop and eat." He slipped off the backpack and dropped it onto a large, flat rock.

"We haven't gone very far!" Mandy protested. "But I am thirsty."

James opened the backpack and hauled a Tupperware container from the depths of the bag. Mandy had put in a rawhide chew for Sunshine and another one for Blackie. There was a plastic bowl and a bottle of water for the dogs, too.

"Yum," said James. "Cheese and lettuce on wholewheat. And a slice of chocolate cake each!"

"And cold orange juice," Mandy said, handing him a bottle. She poured out the water for the dogs. Sunshine wasn't far away. She scampered over and had a drink.

They ate their sandwiches, looking down onto the valley floor. Sunshine lay in the shade of a bush, holding her chew upright between her front paws and gnawing at it with her head on one side. Blackie crunched his chew up in seconds and wandered off to nose around in the undergrowth.

"Look over there!" James pointed. "Someone on an ATV is waving. . . ."

Mandy looked across to the field on their left. "It's Jack Spiller!" she said. She waved back. "He must be checking on the Syke Farm sheep. Look, he's got Tess with him! Let's go over to the farm."

James picked up the backpack and heaved it onto his back. When they neared the perimeter fence of Syke Farm, he put Blackie on his leash and suggested Mandy do the same with Sunshine.

"Sunshine might not have seen a lamb before. You don't know how she'll react," he said.

"You're right," Mandy agreed. Sunshine walked at her heels down the hill and into the farmyard, where Mandy spotted Jack's wife, Maggie, and their children, feeding the chickens.

Blackie barked, alerting Maggie to their arrival. Jenny, the Spillers' six-year-old daughter, waved, then went back to scattering the grain on the ground. A few hens were pecking about, scratching in the dust and darting forward, making baby Adam chuckle. The little boy was named after Dr. Adam, who'd helped with his unexpected arrival.

"Hi, Mrs. Spiller! Hello, Jenny!" Mandy called.

"Hello, Mandy and James!" Maggie stroked Blackie's glossy head, then looked down at the poodle, who was sitting on Mandy's foot. "And who's this?"

"This is Sunshine," Mandy said. "She's a stray. We're keeping her till we find her owner."

"Baa," said Adam, tottering over with an outstretched hand. "Baa!"

"No, Adam." James laughed. "Sunshine is not a *lamb*. She's a dog!"

"It's her pretty woolly coat," said Maggie. "She does look a little like a lamb!"

"How's everything going?" Mandy asked, gently disengaging Adam's hand from Sunshine's ear. "On the farm, I mean?"

Maggie picked the two-year-old up and perched him on her hip. "We're doing well," she said. "We've had two more sets of twin lambs, so that's good news for Ken."

"Frida," Jenny piped up, pointing toward the barn.

"What about Frida, Jenny?" Mandy asked. Jenny had scattered the last of her feed for the hens. She looked up at Mandy with grave, dark eyes.

"She's sad," Jenny announced. "Frida isn't eating."

"I'm afraid that's true," Maggie said. "Jack says that stubborn old ewe is just not herself."

"Can we go and see her?" asked James, holding on tight to Blackie, who was inching closer to an aggressive-looking rooster.

"Sure," Maggie said. "I'm going to the village now, so I'll leave you to it. Say hello to your mom and dad for me, won't you? And good luck with the poodle!"

"Thanks, Mrs. Spiller. Bye, Jenny. Bye, Adam," said Mandy.

"Bye," James said.

They left both dogs in the farmyard, sitting side by side under a tree. Mandy pushed open the big, wooden door of the barn. Instantly, the sound of bleating filled her ears. Newborn lambs tottered about in their stalls, butting at their mothers' udders for milk and falling over on their uncertain, skinny legs. Mandy stopped briefly to stroke a little one asleep in the straw before heading over to Frida's pen.

The ewe was standing up, facing the corner of her stall. Her head hung sadly. Mandy thought she seemed

even thinner than before, even though her fleece was starting to grow back.

"Oh, Frida!" Mandy breathed. The sheep turned her head, then looked away and went back to staring at nothing at all.

"Look at her!" James exclaimed. "She must miss her own lambs. She looks so . . . different!"

"She's lost weight, I can tell," Mandy said.

Outside, Blackie had begun to bark. "We'd better get the dogs and go back for our bikes," James said. "There's nothing we can do for Frida, after all. We can't bring her lambs back to life."

"You're right," Mandy said, turning away from Frida's stall with a stab of hopelessness. "But I don't think I've ever seen an animal look so miserable or so lonely! I wish we could do something to help her!"

Back at the cottage, James had just begun to unpack the picnic things when the bell in the reception area sounded. Sunshine, tired out from her run back down the hill, had been fast asleep on the rug under the kitchen table. But she suddenly sprang up as if electrified and started rushing around in circles. Mandy had both her hands under running water at the sink. Sunshine seized the hem of her jeans and began to tug hard.

"Hey! Sunshine!" Mandy laughed. "Calm down!" She hopped on one leg to keep her balance — she had been rinsing mud off the sides of her sneaker.

"I'll get it," said James, when the bell rang again. Sunshine kept tugging at Mandy's jeans, so she took off the other sneaker and padded along in her socks to the clinic with the poodle circling her feet.

"Who can that be?" said Dr. Adam, emerging from the storeroom. "We're closed until five P.M. today."

Mandy and her father joined James at the door to the waiting room. Amelia Ponsonby was just about to press the bell a third time.

"Ah," said Dr. Adam, "Mrs. Ponsonby's come for her deworming medication. I'll get it."

"Hello, Mrs. P!" James beamed. Sunshine squeezed past and dashed into the reception area, dancing around with her tail wagging madly.

"Oh, James! I didn't think there was anybody around," said Mrs. Ponsonby, clearly put out by the wait. "And what a *rambunctious* little dog this is!" She glared at Sunshine, who was investigating her straw sandal.

"She gets very excited by doorbells," Mandy explained, kneeling down and pulling Sunshine into her arms. The poodle stood up and licked Mandy's face lovingly.

"Really! So unlike my Pandora — who is, as you know, such a *lady*!" Mrs. Ponsonby declared. "Have you thought about giving this poodle a lesson or two in obedience, dear? You might find it easier to take care of her if you offer her a bit of training."

James spoke up. "Actually, she's really well behaved."

"Hmm," said Mrs. Ponsonby. "In that case, I wonder why she hasn't been taught to behave when someone rings a doorbell?"

Mandy got to her feet. "My father is bringing you —"

"I'm just here for my deworming medicine," Mrs. Ponsonby interrupted. "Could you call your father, dear? Or your mother? I haven't much time, you see."

"Yes, Mrs. Ponsonby." Mandy smiled. "My dad will be here in a minute. Say hello to Pandora and Toby for me!"

"Yes, thank you, dear," said the large, elderly lady, flapping a lace-edged handkerchief in front of her face. "Oh, this heat!" she murmured, as Mandy left the room.

"Dad," Mandy said on her way back to the kitchen, "Mrs. P's in a hurry."

"Coming!" called Dr. Adam.

Mandy began mopping her wet sneaker with a piece of paper towel. "I wonder why Sunshine is so upset by bells and horns."

"Maybe she was hit by a car, or a bicycle," James suggested, placing the empty Tupperware container in the dishwasher.

"But she's not *scared*," Mandy said thoughtfully. "In fact, she seems excited and happy when she hears a knock or a bell. And Mrs. Ponsonby's right — she's so well trained in every other way, why did her owners let her misbehave around loud noises?"

"It is a little strange," James agreed.

"Let's try an experiment," Mandy said. "You ride your bike up and down the road, but out of sight. Ring your bell every few seconds and I'll watch what she does. That way, we'll know if it's any old ringing she reacts to or sounds that are only happening in the house."

James looked at Blackie. He was stretched out on the cool floor, asleep. The big Labrador had snoozed soundly through all the commotion of Mrs. Ponsonby's arrival next door, while Sunshine was *still* looking around expectantly.

"I'll leave Blackie with you," he said.

When he had left, Mandy put on her sneakers and kept a watchful eye on Sunshine. The poodle sat looking up at her, her bright little eyes eager and alert. At the slightest noise her head cocked and her eyes darted around. Suddenly, she flew into action, turning in circles. Mandy stood still. She hadn't heard a thing, but

Sunshine was frantic! She rushed around and then, when Mandy didn't move, the poodle snatched at the hem of her jeans and began to pull.

Mandy turned her head and sat still, looking in the other direction. She wondered if, by refusing to react, the poodle would lose interest and calm down. That was the best way to train dogs not to be afraid of certain things, by encouraging them to take a cue from their owner's behavior and act as if nothing was going on. Instead, Sunshine grew even more frantic. She tried to tug Mandy toward the door, yapping encouragement. Her tail was wagging furiously. Her bright little eyes were trained on Mandy's face, as though she were trying to communicate something. Now that Mandy was studying her closely, there was no sign of fear or anxiety. Instead, Sunshine was alert and excited in a positive way. What could it mean?

"OK!" Mandy said. She slipped on Sunshine's leash. "Come on, then. Let's go!"

As soon as the door was open, Sunshine took off, with Mandy running as fast as she could to keep up. Sunshine's black button nose worked hard and it didn't take her long to locate James, who was just across the road from the clinic parking lot.

She sat down, panting and triumphant. Mandy patted her lovingly.

"Sunshine *loves* sounds!" she said, laughing. "She's not scared of noises, she just wants everyone to know that they're happening. Doorbells, telephones, doors slamming, alarm clocks, it's all the same to her. It's like she thinks I can't hear them myself, and she needs to let me know they're going on!"

"She's the funniest, sweetest little —" James began, stroking Sunshine, but Mandy interrupted him.

"That's it!" she cried.

"What?" said James.

"She's been trained to respond to noises!" Mandy said. "Sunshine must be a hearing dog!"

Nine

James looked blank.

"They're like guide dogs for deaf people, rather than blind people. They act as a deaf person's ears, letting them know when their alarm clock goes off or the doorbell rings. Or if there's a fire alarm," Mandy explained. "They can be much smaller than other assistance dogs because they don't have to carry anything or lead their owners around."

James looked at Sunshine with admiration in his eyes. "You're right! It makes sense the way she reacts whenever she hears a noise. It's the only thing she doesn't seem to be well trained at — except now, it seems it's the thing she's *best* trained at!"

It was a complicated way of putting it, but Mandy knew what he meant. She looked at Sunshine, who looked back at her with her pretty, apricot-colored ears pricked up. Then she licked Mandy's nose. "Come on, let's go and tell Mom and Dad," said Mandy.

Sunshine trotted beside Mandy on her leash, her head high. She always looked so proud, Mandy thought. Maybe that was because Sunshine knew what a clever and special dog she was.

Mandy's parents were in the kitchen. Dr. Adam was peeling carrots and singing. Dr. Emily was reading the evening newspaper. "There you are," she said. "We wondered why you'd left Blackie asleep in the reception area."

"Mom! Dad!" Mandy burst out. "Sunshine's a hearing dog!"

Dr. Emily blinked. "What makes you think that?"

James stepped over Blackie, who opened one eye and yawned. He sat down and explained their theory. Dr. Adam stopped peeling and came over to listen.

"Why didn't I think of that?" He looked very excited. "Mandy, look up the Hearing Dogs Association on the computer. They'll have a Web site. If you're lucky, you might find . . ."

But Mandy was already on her way. She rushed into the den, James on her heels. Sunshine wasn't far behind.

"It does seem to explain her rather unusual behavior," Dr. Emily said, following them into the room.

Mandy's fingers flew over the keys, searching for the Hearing Dogs Association. Up it came, with a bold and colorful Web site. There were several sections to choose from. She looked for a heading about missing dogs, but there wasn't anything related.

"Try 'Dog Partnerships,'" James suggested. "Sunshine might be listed there with a picture."

The screen page was devoted to hearing dogs and their owners. There were photographs of men and women with their working dogs. Mandy scrolled down, feeling optimistic. There were dozens of photographs of gorgeous dogs, from Jack Russell terriers to Labradors and big, goofy-looking mixed breeds. Mandy wanted to read about each dog in turn, but there was no time to spare. There was one special dog she had to find first.

And there, suddenly, was Sunshine's beloved little face, looking back at her!

"Wow!" James yelled, making Mandy jump.

"Sunshine!" said Dr. Emily.

The caption beneath the photo read: HEARING DOG OF THE YEAR: BOO, A TWO-YEAR-OLD APRICOT POODLE, OWNED BY SALLY WEBSTER OF WALTON.

Mandy was so overcome, her eyes filled with hot tears of pride. "Not Sunshine, Mom," she said, swallowing hard. "Boo! Her name is Boo. How cute! It sounds happy, so it suits her personality."

"Read what else it says," James urged.

Mandy read aloud: *"Boo is a bright and enthusiastic miniature poodle who began her training at a year old. Having discovered Boo's love of fruit, the treat was used as a reward as she went through her paces, learning and adapting to her new life quicker than anyone had expected. Just before her second birthday, she was placed with Ms. Webster, a partnership that worked perfectly for both owner and dog. UPDATE: Very sadly, Boo was lost on a walk across the Dales a week ago. Her collar was found but Boo had not been microchipped. If anyone has seen her, please contact the organization urgently. Boo is desperately missed by Sally, not just as a hearing dog but as her best friend and constant companion."*

Mandy looked up at her mother, blinking back the tears that threatened to spill down her cheeks. "Poor Sally Webster," she said.

Dr. Emily shook her head. "Yes, but this is *great* news, honey. The puzzle is solved, and Sally can have her dog back." She looked at her watch. "It's too late to call the association now. We'll call first thing in the morning."

"Yes," said Mandy, stroking Boo's head, wondering if the poodle had been missing her owner as much as Sally had missed her. Boo had been cheerful and loyal, but there was no doubt in Mandy's mind that she would be over the moon with joy to see Sally again!

Mandy dialed the number of the Hearing Dogs Association soon after eight o'clock on Tuesday morning. She got a voice mail message that told her to call back at nine. The hour passed quickly — she brushed Boo's coat until the curls turned to peachy fluff — and the little dog looked magnificent. "It's for Sally," she told the poodle, pushing her own sadness aside. "You're going home today, I'm sure of it."

Finally, Dr. Adam was able to get through to the Hearing Dogs Association. He explained why he was calling. "Can I have Ms. Webster's telephone number?" he asked. Mandy heard him say, "Oh, I see. Yes, thank you," before he put down the phone.

"Did you get her number?" Mandy said.

"We have to wait until Sally Webster gets in touch with the association," he reported. "She has a special light on her receiver, as she can't hear the telephone ringing — and, of course, Boo isn't there to alert her."

"Oh," said Mandy. Just then, the phone rang and Dr. Adam reached for it. *That was quick*, thought Mandy.

"Hello?" said her dad tentatively. "Yes? OK. No problem. I'm on my way."

"More problems at Syke Farm?" Mandy asked, frowning.

Her father nodded. "One of Ken's ewes is in trouble. It looks like another multiple birth. Want to come along?"

"Oh . . ." Mandy chewed her lip. "But what about Sally?"

"It might be a while before she picks up her message," her father pointed out.

"And I'm sure you'll be back before she can arrange to come over," her mom added.

"OK." Mandy started for the stairs. "I'll get dressed." She gave Boo a hug and ruffled her fluffy head. "I'll be back soon," she promised.

The morning sun was drinking up the dew, drying the glistening fields they passed on the way to the farm. Lambs scampered around while their mothers pulled at the grass. Mandy thought of Frida. She would ask Jack for some feed and visit her, if there was time.

Tess was lying in the shade of a bush in the front yard at Syke Farm. She barked at Dr. Adam's Land Rover, then went slinking away around the side of the house, out of sight. Mandy wished Ken would come home soon. The poor dog seemed so lost without her owner around!

Her father headed quickly for the barn, swinging his black bag. Mandy went after Tess. She came hesitantly when Mandy called and lay down to be pet, resting her ice-cold nose in Mandy's palm. Her sad, deep brown eyes spoke volumes.

Jack Spiller and Mandy's dad were deep in conversation at the door of the barn when Mandy joined them. Her father looked grim.

"It's been too long," Mr. Spiller was saying. "She's having a bad time."

"Lead the way," said Dr. Adam.

Mandy padded softly behind them. She dreaded what she would see. Frida's struggle to give birth — and her poor twin lambs — had been bad enough to witness. Jack Spiller, though much younger than Ken, seemed exhausted. He looked as though he had been up all night, and there was hay in his hair. Mandy feared the worst.

The ewe was scrambling around in the stall, as though trying to get away from the pain in her swollen belly. Her eyes were bulging, big and golden brown. She bleated pitifully, then stamped her hoof and shook her head from side to side. Mandy's heart began to thud. She looked as distressed as Frida had been when she was trying to give birth.

Dr. Adam stepped into the pen and ran his hands over the ewe. "You're right, Jack, there's definitely more than one in here, but they're tangled and I don't think she has the strength to get them out by herself. I'm going to have to do a Caesarean," he said.

Mandy shuddered. She knew that this was a risky procedure that involved her father having to anesthetize the sheep and perform a surgical operation to remove the lambs by hand.

"Mandy, can you open my bag and hand me a syringe?" her father asked. "And Jack, could you get me a bucket of warm water so I can scrub up?"

"Sure," said Jack, striding toward the barn door.

Mandy climbed into the stall beside the ewe and pulled on a pair of disposable gloves. She kneeled down, took a deep breath, and waited for her father's instruction.

"Please, let the lambs be OK," she whispered. But her father looked concerned as he tipped a bottle and stabbed the needle through the cork, filling his syringe.

Mandy began to feel extremely warm. Looking up, she noticed that Jack had fixed a fan heater into the rafters of the barn. It hung there, blowing a warm breeze onto the back of Mandy's neck. Dr. Adam was holding the ewe between his legs. He quickly swabbed a place along her spine with antiseptic, then gave her a shot of anesthetic between two of her vertebrae. Then the ewe lay down sleepily, folding at the knees.

"Good girl," muttered Dr. Adam. "You're going to be an excellent patient."

"Why?" Mandy asked.

"Because she's very, very tired," her father answered. The ewe rolled over onto her side and gave a big sigh. "Now she can't feel anything much at all."

"Oh, good," said Mandy.

"Now, sweetheart," he went on, "I'm going to need your help. Pass me the cordless electric razor, please."

Mandy scrabbled in his bag and handed it over. She watched carefully as patches of the ewe's woolly coat fell away, exposing a neat little area on her tummy about five inches long. At that moment, Jack Spiller appeared, carrying a bucket of clean, soapy warm water.

"Thanks, Jack," Dr. Adam said, plunging his hands into it. When her father had pulled on his sterile gloves, Mandy opened his medical kit again and quickly laid out the tools he would need onto a clean cloth.

The ewe was breathing hard but she lay still, and only her hooves twitched on the hard floor. Mandy looked away as her father made the first cut. When she glanced back, she saw that with his free hand, her father was dabbing the edges around the cut.

A few moments later, he gave a low whistle. "Not twins or triplets, but *four* lambs! Quads!" said Dr. Adam, sounding dumbfounded. "That's rare."

Mandy looked down at the ewe. Four tiny bodies were squeezed up tightly in the stretchy pouch in her side. They lay head to toe, hoof to mouth, their eyes closed.

"Four?" said Jack. "I haven't seen that before. All healthy?"

"All breathing," Dr. Adam reported. "I'm going to need a hand now. They're very small and will need stimulation once they are delivered."

"There's a stack of towels over there," Jack said. "I'll get them."

"Mandy," Dr. Adam said, "you'll have to rub them briskly but gently, just as their mother's tongue would be doing if she were awake."

Mandy was down on her knees in the straw beside her father. Her hands trembled fearfully. She didn't know if she could bear to see the lambs brought out if they weren't OK. When Jack handed her a towel, she opened it, ready to take the first lamb her father gave her.

"One," he said, very gently placing the tiny newborn

into the hammock of her towel. Mandy held the little creature against the warmth of her lap. She rubbed it carefully, feeling the delicate bones beneath the loose-fitting skin. Then she cleared its mouth with the tip of her small finger. The lamb gave a shuddering gasp. It was alive!

"Two," said Dr. Adam, passing the next one to Jack Spiller.

Mandy laid the first lamb on the straw. Now she accepted its sibling and rubbed it warm and dry. Jack Spiller took the fourth. "All alive!" he said jubilantly. "Great job, Adam, you *and* Mandy!"

Mandy's father was concentrating on stitching up the ewe. Jack laid the two lambs down, then redirected the heater so that it spilled warmth onto the quadruplets. Mandy found that she was crying. Tears ran down her cheeks, but she couldn't tell if they were tears of relief or happiness. The lambs were so small, so helpless, yet so determined. They wiggled and gasped, looking for milk, looking for their mother.

"It's bottle time!" said Jack Spiller. "Mandy, can you help feed?"

Mandy smiled. "I'd love to," she said. She stood up, and found that her knees were wobbly — just like the lambs'!

*   *   *

Half an hour later, Mandy sat on the floor in Dora Janeki's kitchen with Maggie and Jack Spiller, the four lambs divided between them.

"Eeny, Meeny, Miny, and Mo," she declared. "That's what we'll call them — if Ken doesn't mind, that is!"

Maggie laughed. "They're good names," she said. She rubbed the back of a lamb that had finished a whole bottle of formula and it gave a tiny belch.

The door opened and Dr. Adam came in. "Thanks for your help," he said, beaming at Mandy. "You handled that really well. And now all I need is a cup of tea!"

Maggie got up. "Of course," she said. "Thanks for coming out, Adam. I'll put the kettle on."

Mandy felt herself relax. She drew the lambs toward her along the floor and put her arms around them. They smelled of wool and straw and sweet milk. They were adorable!

Ten

That night, Mandy slept with Boo tucked up close to her chest. Boo's owner would come and get her tomorrow. Mandy was still going to miss the cuddly little dog, but now that she knew Boo was going home to someone who truly loved her and would take excellent care of her, she found she didn't mind quite so much.

On their arrival back from Syke Farm, Dr. Emily had relayed a message from the Hearing Dogs Association. Sally Webster had been in touch. She was ecstatic about Boo having been found and planned to get her first thing the next morning. So Mandy said her good-byes, stroking Boo and planting small kisses on her soft ears.

In return, Boo looked long and hard into Mandy's eyes, and gave her the gentlest of licks before curling up with her head on Mandy's shoulder and falling fast asleep.

Boo heard her owner's car before Mandy did. They were in the living room, waiting. Mandy was looking out of the window, her curiosity making her impatient. Then the poodle started dashing around in circles, barking. She jumped up at Mandy, scrabbling with her sharp little claws against Mandy's bare legs.

"Ouch! Stop it, Boo!" Mandy pleaded. She saw a green Land Rover pull up at the front of Animal Ark. Once more, Boo's ears had beat hers. "OK, let's go say hello." She followed Boo through to the reception area.

Sally Webster was young, which somehow Mandy hadn't expected. She was also very pretty, with thick, bouncy red curls and a heart-shaped face. She hurried forward to shake Mandy's hand before sinking to her knees to hug Boo.

The dog was quivering with pleasure and letting out little yelps of excitement. This wasn't just regular friendliness; this time, there was no doubt in Mandy's mind that Boo's real owner had arrived.

Sally gathered her into her arms and covered her with kisses. "Oh, my baby!" she said. "Don't ever go off chasing rabbits again, do you hear?"

Mandy watched with a lump in her throat.

At last, Sally stood up. Her eyes were wet. "Thank you," she said. "I thought I'd never see her again."

Mandy smiled. She wasn't sure whether she should speak or not. Could Sally hear her? Her voice had been rather flat and strange-sounding. So Mandy nodded and Sally laughed.

"You can talk," she said. "I'm a good lip-reader. Just face me when you have something to say, OK?"

"OK." Mandy grinned. Her parents arrived and Mandy did the introductions. Sally told them how grateful she was, and offered to pay for Boo's care while she had been staying at Animal Ark.

"Oh, no," said Dr. Adam. "We loved having her. She's a great little dog."

"Sally," Mandy said, "my friend James has helped me a lot with Boo. I know he'd like to say good-bye to her. Will you walk with me to his house? He doesn't live very far away. We could take Boo."

"Sure," Sally said. She wore blue jeans and sneakers, and she had a cardigan tied around her waist, which she took off and slipped her arms into. Then she put on her dog's collar and leash. They were tan-colored, well-worn and soft-looking. "Ready," she declared with a smile.

Mandy walked alongside Sally, who held Boo's leash. Now that Sally was back in her life, Boo's attention was totally focused on her owner. Her ears were pricked, alert for sounds that might signal danger. Mandy watched her with admiration.

"Welford is great," Sally said as they walked along. "It's such a pretty place. I haven't been here before."

"We wondered why you hadn't heard the interview on Dales Radio," Mandy told her, pausing to look at Sally as she spoke.

"I wish I had," she answered, leading Boo across a road. "None of my friends or family heard it, either."

"You might find that Boo is pretty famous now!" Mandy warned, remembering the poodle's warm reception at the village hospital. "But I guess she's used to having a public profile, thanks to the Hearing Dogs Association's Web site."

"It's great, isn't it?" Sally enthused. "I was so thrilled when they picked me to have a hearing dog. Boo's such an important part of my life. She's a great companion, for a start, and she helps make my life work. She wakes me up in the morning, because I can't hear the alarm clock. . . ."

"She woke me up, too!" Mandy laughed. But she'd forgotten to look at Sally, and so she hadn't read a word Mandy said.

". . . she tells me when someone is approaching the house or at the door — and once, when my smoke alarm went off! Luckily, I'd just burned some toast, but I know I can depend on her to save me in an emergency."

They'd reached the village green and Mandy saw James coming toward them. Blackie was trying to drag him onto the grass and James was resisting strenuously, hauling on the leash.

"Look at that patch of pansies," Sally said. "They've planted them so that they spell out something."

"It says, 'Welcome to Welford,'" Mandy said, looking at Sally. "And here comes James!"

He looked flustered and hot as he tugged his dog over to Mandy and Sally.

"James," Mandy said, "this is Sally Webster, Boo's owner."

"Hello," James said. He leaned over to stroke Boo's head.

Mandy nudged him. "Sally can read lips, so look at her when you talk," she said.

James looked up at Sally and smiled. "We love your dog," he said, speaking a little too loudly.

"Shh," Mandy said with her back to Sally. "There's no need to yell, James. She can't hear you, anyway."

"Thank you," said Sally. "I love her, too. And what a beautiful Labrador," she added, bending down to pet Blackie, who was whimpering excitedly. "I can see that Boo has made some good friends in Welford."

James nodded. They turned back toward Animal Ark. Mandy's heart was heavy as they approached the parking lot. This, at last, would mean good-bye to Sunshine, Peachy, and Boo — all the same remarkable little dog.

Sally opened the passenger door of her Land Rover and Boo jumped in. Sally gave Mandy a warm hug before going around to the other side and climbing in. Mandy kissed the poodle's nose through the open window. "Bye," she said, trying to swallow a big lump in her throat. "Take care of Sally."

"I'll be in touch," Sally told Mandy. "Thank you. We won't forget you, will we, Boo?"

The poodle yapped and put her two front paws up on the dashboard. Mandy smiled. Boo obviously knew exactly where she was going. She stood side by side with James and Blackie as Sally backed out of the parking lot and tooted her horn as she drove away.

"Gone already?" asked Dr. Adam, stepping out of the clinic's main door. "I was just coming to say good-bye."

"Gone already," Mandy said, staring after the car.

Her father put a warm hand on her shoulder. "Good job," he said softly. "That wasn't easy, I know."

"No," said Mandy, stroking Blackie, who was rubbing his cheek against her leg.

"OK. Who's coming with me to lend a hand at Syke Farm? Jack's having a hard time with those four pesky lambs."

"Me!" James said, adding, "Please."

"We should leave Blackie here, then," said Dr. Adam. "Mandy?"

Mandy smiled. There was never time to feel sad for too long at Animal Ark. Animals always needed her help — and really, she could only feel happy that Boo had finally found her home. "Coming!" she declared.

The kitchen at Syke Farm was in chaos. Mandy stood in the open doorway and gasped. Miny and Mo had butted down the makeshift barricade that kept them in a corner of the big room and were skipping around freely, scattering straw as they went. A chair had been overturned and the whole place smelled like a barn, only worse.

"Oh, dear," said James, surveying the scene.

Mandy looked around. "Where are the others?" She turned to James as though he might have the answer. "Eeny and Meeny aren't here!"

Maggie had baby Adam on her hip. She yawned. "I've been up all night with this little guy," she explained. "He's teething and I'm so tired — and Dora's due back today. She's going to have a fit!"

"Don't worry, Mrs. Spiller," Mandy said. "James and I will help. But two of the lambs are missing. . . . They haven't . . . they're not . . ." Mandy couldn't bring herself to say out loud what she feared.

"Oh, no!" Maggie said. "We took two back out to their mom. We're just going to bottle-feed this pair because she can't manage all of them."

Mandy felt herself relax. *What a relief!*

"Where's your dad, Mandy?" asked Maggie.

"Out in the barn with Mr. Spiller," Mandy told her. The lambs bleated insistently, tapping around on their small hooves, lifting their faces in search of milk. "Should I start making lunch for this pair?"

"Thanks. The formula is over by the sink," Maggie said, raising her voice above their noise and making Adam cry. "Give them four ounces each, OK? Clean bottles on the draining board. Thanks!"

She left, and Mandy got to work, boiling a kettle and mixing the formula in a jug for each lamb.

James set out the feeding bottles. "They're so cute and so tiny," he remarked, surveying the chaos. "Who would have thought they could cause so much trouble?"

Mandy laughed and sat on the floor. She handed James a bottle and pulled Mo onto her lap. She could hardly believe she'd seen this boisterous and demanding little creature snuggled limply inside his mother's body.

James was battling to get Miny to take the nipple of the bottle. The more he pushed the rubber tip into her mouth, the louder she bleated. She wouldn't sit on James's lap; she fought to be free until James dropped the bottle and the top came off. The milk puddled on the floor.

"Oh, no!" he said as the lamb, startled, scuttled away.

Mo was sucking so fast the milk streamed out of the corner of his pink mouth and ran all over Mandy's legs. "This isn't very easy," she said.

"It's tricky for humans to feed lambs," James decided. "We need a sheep who knows what to do."

"Well, there's no such thing as a sheep mid-wife," Mandy said. "Unless . . ." A great idea had just popped into her mind. "I wonder if we could get Frida to look after these two? I mean, if their mom hasn't got enough milk for four babies, why can't Frida share some of hers?" She knew it wasn't unknown for other ewes to foster very young lambs, but Frida had lost her lambs several days ago, and was grieving so deeply that she might not want to cooperate. Still, it was worth a try.

James looked up at her. "That's a great idea! But how will we persuade Frida to feed lambs that are not hers?" He caught Miny and carried her back to where the bottle lay.

"She would have recognized her own lambs by their scent. So we'll have to disguise the way Miny and Mo smell," Mandy said.

James gave up trying to feed Miny and set her down on her skinny legs. He started opening cupboard doors in the kitchen cabinets. Behind some glasses, he spotted a bottle of aspirin and a box of bandages. There was also a jar of Mentholyptus rub.

"Will this work?" James asked Mandy, holding up the jar.

"Oh, yes! That's perfect!" Mandy said. "When we were in Manitoba, they used the same kind of rub on the polar bear's fur to trick her into thinking the orphaned cubs were hers. It smells so strong that it disguises both scents so the bears think they smell the same. It worked perfectly."

"Great," James said. "Let's pen them up as best we can and go and ask your dad."

Mo and Miny were barricaded into a corner of the kitchen. Miny protested loudly, her tiny tail bobbing up and down, while Mo folded at the knees and closed his eyes.

James and Mandy ran over to the barn and consulted with Dr. Adam.

"Frida's not a young mother," he said. "She's very smart when it comes to looking after lambs. But I suppose she could be fooled into thinking they belong to her. Give it a try, we've got nothing to lose."

Back in Dora's kitchen, Mandy woke Mo by lifting him as gently as she could. Miny was still hungry and opened her mouth to bleat at James for food. She was all legs, flailing around in his arms as James carried her across the yard to the barn. As he set her down, Mandy advised that he keep a tight hold of the lambs at the scruff of their necks. She put Mo down beside Miny.

Mandy dipped two fingers into the jar and smeared the bright green ointment over the lambs' spines and under their tails. Mo cried pitifully, and Mandy felt mean.

"Poor Mo," she said. "I know, it smells very strange." She worked as quickly as she could, rubbing in the strong-smelling medication while Miny and Mo struggled to be free of James's grip.

"Quick," he gasped. "I can't hold them much longer."

"OK," Mandy said, flinging the jar aside. "Let's take them in to Frida."

They carried the lambs, still bleating angrily, to Frida's stall. The ewe didn't even look up at the sound of their noisy approach. Mandy stepped into her stall and set down the tiny, snowy bundle. James lowered Miny down onto the straw, and Frida's nose began to twitch. She turned and took a step toward the lambs, lowering her head and breathing hard. Mo stood up and wobbled with great determination toward Frida, butting at her belly for milk. Frida whirled around, her eyes wide. With her nose, she investigated every inch of Miny and Mo in turn, while Mandy bit her thumbnail. It seemed to be taking forever for Frida to decide if she would accept the lambs.

"Oh, yikes," James whispered, "she's not going to accept them. . . ."

Mandy saw Frida's nose lingering under the tails of each of the lambs, then, suddenly, she lay down and rolled onto her side, allowing Mo to find her milk.

James clutched at Mandy, squeezing her shoulder hard in his excitement. "We *did* it!" he cried.

"Shh! Wait," she cautioned him.

But when Miny began to drink as well, and Mandy saw the ewe rest her head and close her eyes, Mandy climbed out of the pen and began jumping up and down. "We did it!" she sang. "We did it!"

"Did what?" said a gruff voice behind them. Mandy whirled around. Dora Janeki had come into the barn, carrying a battered leather suitcase. She looked very surprised to see Mandy and James leaping up and down. "And what, may I ask, is that strange smell?"

"Um . . ." James began, but Dr. Adam had spotted Dora and he came over and took the suitcase from her.

"Dora! Welcome home," he said.

"Adam," she said, looking from one face to another, "what's going on? Where's Ken?"

"Your brother has had pneumonia," Dr. Adam explained. "But he's fine now and recovering in Walton Hospital. Jack Spiller has been keeping an eye on things here."

"Goodness," said Dora, turning pale. "Is Ken —"

"He's fine," Dr. Adam promised. "In fact, he can come home tomorrow. How was the anniversary party?"

"Very nice," Dora said absently. She looked around. "What *is* that smell?"

"Frida's twin lambs died, Mrs. Janeki," Mandy explained. "And then another ewe had four lambs and couldn't feed them all. James and I have just helped two of the quads to nurse with Frida by disguising their scent with Mentholyptus rub."

Dora Janeki blinked in astonishment. "Did you? Good job. Quads, you say? Adam, is this true?"

"Yep," said Dr. Adam, leading Dora out of the barn. "All healthy and strong."

"Honestly, I go away for five days and miss everything! I really *must* get myself a cell phone!" Dora muttered, shaking her head.

Mandy took another peek at Frida. The big ewe seemed content at last. Mandy had a feeling that she knew these weren't her own lambs, but they needed a mother, and that was something Frida could provide for them. Mandy's mom was right in a way: Animals didn't grieve exactly like humans, but these two lambs in need of fostering had definitely brought Frida out of her mourning. Miny and Mo fed happily, and Frida's tail bobbed up and down. Smiling, Mandy followed her father and Dora outside. Just then, Tess came streaking across the yard, her tail streaming behind, and flung herself against Dora. Boo hadn't been the only dog waiting for a happy reunion with her owner.

Everything had worked out perfectly!

Eleven

Mandy was up early on Easter Sunday. She'd dreamed of Boo and woke up to find herself reaching for the familiar warmth of the poodle's curly coat. Trying not to feel too sad, she jumped up, dressed quickly, and went leaping down the stairs.

The kitchen was bustling with activity. Grandma Hope had arrived, wearing a new hat, and Mandy's mother was putting chocolate eggs into various plastic bags.

"Two bags for you," she said as Mandy came in. "And two for James. Where *is* James?"

"Hello, Gran," Mandy said, planting a kiss on her soft cheek.

"Here!" James announced, coming through the back door. "Hello."

"Hi, James," said Dr. Emily. "Here are your bags. Mandy, grab some breakfast. Then you and James can go off and hide the eggs."

"I plan to fill up on chocolate today," Mandy said. "It's a special day."

"Do you have your route planned out?" Mandy's grandmother asked. "You know exactly where to hide them?"

"Exactly," James assured her.

"Get going, then." Dr. Emily flapped her hands. "But try not to eat any yet!"

Mandy and James set out. Low clouds glowered from a dark sky, and Mandy felt disappointed. It was still early, though. Mandy and James walked briskly, locating each of their hiding places and making certain the eggs were not too easily visible. When the bags were empty, they turned for home.

Dorothy Hope smiled as they came into the kitchen. "*Now* you deserve a reward!" She chuckled. She produced two large chocolate bunnies wearing bow ties. "Thank you for your help, and happy Easter!"

"Oh, Gran!" said Mandy. "Thanks!" As a vegetarian, she wouldn't normally eat rabbit, but chocolate versions were utterly delicious!

*   *   *

By the time the village green had filled with people, the sun was beaming from a cheery blue sky. The excited squeals of children mingled with the peal of the bells from the church. Mrs. Ponsonby was standing in the middle of the grass with her Pekingese, Pandora, under her arm and Toby on his leash.

"I can't quite read what it says," she was saying to Ernie Bell, bending over and squinting at the pansy bed. "Are you sure it says *Welford*?"

Mandy rolled her eyes at James. The bed looked beautiful. The pansies had turned their faces to the sun and glowed a bright white. Walter Pickard looked very proud! Mandy spotted Gabriel the miniature pony walking across the green, a garland of flowers around his neck. Jenny Spiller was sitting up very straight in the saddle, beaming. Tania waved to Mandy, then stopped to chide Gabriel for trying to snack on the blooms he was wearing.

"Look!" James said.

Mandy looked where he was pointing. Dora Janeki, her arm linked through her brother's, was leading the most unusual pet: a *lamb*! She held Miny on a leash made from a length of rope. Mo was also on a leash, but danced along on his spindly legs beside Ken, who looked pale but cheerful.

"Easter lambs!" exclaimed someone in the crowd.

Miny kicked up her heels, as if she knew she was the center of attention.

James had a streak of melted chocolate on his chin. "I'll never eat chocolate again," he groaned, rubbing his tummy. "Why did you let me eat the entire chocolate bunny? Couldn't you have just let me have the ears?"

But Mandy wasn't really listening. She had spotted someone she'd been looking out for all morning, hoping they'd come to share the village celebrations. Sally

Webster, with Boo trotting beside her, was threading her way through the crowd toward them. She was talking to the poodle, who paused, her ears pricked, and looked around. Then she spotted Mandy — and Sally let her go.

A blur of apricot-colored fluff came racing toward Mandy. Her ears — the best pair of ears in the world — flapped as she ran, and her tail whirred like an electric hand mixer. Mandy bent down to catch the poodle in her arms, and had her face licked again and again. There was no question that she recognized Mandy, and even though Boo was dedicated to looking after her owner forever, she had a very special place in her heart for the person who had cared for her while she was lost.

"I knew you wouldn't forget me!" said Mandy, choking back happy tears. "The best and cleverest dog in the world. Happy Easter!"